Star-Shot

I drigolion Tan-y-Castell, o dan ac uwchben y dŵr.

Star-shot

mary-ann constantine

SEREN

Seren is the book imprint of
Poetry Wales Press Ltd.
57 Nolton Street, Bridgend, Wales, CF31 3AE
www.serenbooks.com
facebook.com/SerenBooks
twitter@SerenBooks

ISBN: 978-1-78172-264-0
ebook: 978-1-78172-271-8
Kindle: 978-1-78172-278-7

A CIP record for this title is available from the British Library.

The publisher acknowledges the financial assistance of the Welsh Books
Council.

Printed by Latimer Trend, Plymouth.

In names for nostoc (as supposed to be shed from the stars): *star-jelly, star-slime, star-slough, star-slubber, star-slutch*: also *star-fallen, star-falling*, and STAR-SHOT *n*.

(OED: sv STAR *n.*[1] Compounds 8b.)

Some philosophers, not giving themselves time to examine into this phenomenon, imagined them to have been generated in the clouds, and showered on earth; but had they but traced them to the next pond, they would have found a better solution of the difficulty.

Thomas Pennant, 'Frog', *British Zoology*, 1766.

Mary-Ann Constantine's short stories have appeared over a number of years in *New Welsh Review* and *Planet*. She has published two previous collections of stories,*The Breathing* (Planet, 2008) and *All the Souls* (Seren, 2013).

The Cardiff of this story is an unreal place; an out-of-kilter version of the real thing. All characters, institutions and situations are entirely fictional.

Words and phrases in Welsh are translated in the glossary.

1.

She has piled up her dark red hair with a clip, so the building can see the nape of her neck. She puts her bag on the bench beside her and watches the students scattered across the neat grass in the unexpected February sun. They sit and they sprawl; their bodies relax. But she is taut and tense as a dancer, painfully self-aware. Behind her, masked by branches, are dark windows, thick white pillars: a civic, foursquare, symmetrical gaze. The sun brightens everything; it sharpens edges. She slowly loosens a soft cotton scarf from around her neck and sits resolutely facing the town centre, the traffic. She eats her lunch and pretends she cannot feel it. But today, she knows, she will go back to work content; she has its full attention. She hates being ignored.

Deep down Myra will admit she is still a little embarrassed, if not confused, by the whole thing. Not the pull of desire itself: a flame is a flame is a flame, she thinks, at least till it goes out. But the object, so massive, so important. She would have thought herself susceptible to quite other forms. Lost churches, empty warehouses, even some of the new stuff, the big projects, all curves and glass and national slate, blatant but beautiful, mobile pigeon-purples and greys. But early twentieth-century, Portland stone, with the power and glory of the nineteenth still running in its white veins? At least, she thinks defensively, at least it's not a multi-storey car park, or a shopping precinct, or a bank – my god, if it had been a bank. It's a public institution, civic-minded. It intends well.

She is also relieved to have grown out of the castle, not even a proper castle, and there is nothing romantic even about the proper ones if you stop for a moment to consider them. Barracks. An empty threat. She exempts the stone animals from her scorn, however. They are too much part of her childhood, and she can still recite them, walking from town, with her mum, towards the river. Their frightening eyes. Lions, lynx, lioness, bear, seal, apes. And the anteater, or is it an aardvark, she can never remember which.

The new spring sun is lovely on her face and neck. She has a vague sense of crocuses and a squirrel off to the left. Next time, she thinks, she might have to bring sun-cream. At last she checks her phone to see if her time is nearly up. It is. Tensing, she removes her sunglasses and rises from the bench, passing the bronze statue of the pensive little girl and walking out of the patch of park to meet the building's gaze. The shock of it will carry her most of the fifteen-minute walk through the traffic and the shoppers-under-glass, through the derelict patches and building sites, over the railway bridge, back to work.

2.

His legs take the pale steps with their usual loping energy, but he carries the plastic box in his hands like one of the three kings at a nativity play. Awkwardly, almost tenderly: *Aur a thus a myrr*. And then he is through the entrance and in the big cool hall with scores of people holding leaflets and children, moving in all directions around him. He cuts through without seeing them, makes for the enquiry desk, and tells them who he is, why he is there, giving them the name of the person he had spoken to the day before. And waits, patiently, while the woman phones through. He holds the box more closely into his body now, and lets the confusion of the crowd wash over him, so focused, so intent, he hardly hears it. She puts the phone down and asks him to sign the visitors' book, which he does without letting go of his plastic container; an illegible scrawl. Then again, printed, rather childishly: Theo Evans. She'll be here very soon, says the woman at the desk handing him a security tag, if you don't mind waiting there's a place over there you... I don't mind standing, he says. I don't mind at all. And he stands, tall, thin, pale-haired and crumpled-looking. His attitude, as always, is one of faint but benign surprise.

3.

The three-way device drives him mad; it refuses to click, and Teddy instinctively jerks his arms and legs so as to send the straps flying in all directions. A small arm gets free. Dan puts down the rucksack and, this time, crouching in front of the pushchair, gives the task his complete attention, ignoring his son's engaging talk. He aligns the two top pieces of plastic one over the other and fishes the third from underneath a wriggling leg. Then, very deliberately, he slides the pieces together. They click. Beautiful. Teddy is strapped in. He goes back into the house and stands in the kitchen blankly for a minute. Remembers the list. Remembers the envelope. Checks his pocket for his phone. Pulls the front door to and then checks the black bag hanging off the handles of the buggy. Nappies. Wipes. Beaker. Puffy corn snacks. Jar of cheating food, organic. Plastic spoon. Bib. Change of clothes. Ah; no. No change of clothes.

He feels in his jacket pocket for the house keys, opens the stiff blue door with a practised twist and a shove of his shoulder and goes up to Teddy's room where, by some miracle, he lays his hands immediately on what he needs. He glances through the window at the restless tree in the back yard and in spite of the sunshine adds a small red jumper to the bundle. He is halfway downstairs when he has a flash of revelation: the bottle, oh the bottle, the bottle. And then: is there a clean one? Or will I have to? He has been trying to leave the house for twenty-five minutes. He has been trying, and trying hard, to stay calm. The child begins to fuss and strain outside the front door. The bottle is clean; the bottle is sterilised. *Haleliwia*. Let us go then, you and I. Three bumps backwards down the steps to the gate. Goodbye, small terraced house with the dark-blue door. They turn into a street lit up with early spring, full of cats and blossom and postmen, bikes and crisp packets and all the things that make streets wonderful when one of you is very small. He starts to look forward to his coffee.

4.

Theo can now wander through the natural history galleries with his hands deep in his jacket pockets. His plastic box is with them somewhere in the depths, being taken care of.

They will send a sample to the labs and they will get back to him, probably by email, in a fortnight to three weeks. But he thinks he might come back anyway, if he can get away. He enjoyed talking to the woman with the grey ponytail, he had quickly been able to make her laugh with his snippets of Morton and Pennant and Fort, all off pat by now, they go round in his head the whole time. *I shall here set down my Remarks, says Morton, upon the gelatinous Body call'd Star-gelly, Star-shot, or Star-fall'n, so named because vulgarly believ'd to fall from a Star, or to be the Recrement of the Meteor which is called the Falling or Shooting Star.* Which is nonsense, as everyone knows, because with his own eyes he, Morton, *saw a Coddymoddy* – that is, says Theo, a kind of gull – *shot down to the ground, that on her Fall … disgorg'd a heap of Half-Digested Earthworms, much resembling that Gelly called Star-shot.* And Mr Pennant, a little later, quite agrees.

But Fort, of course, wants the stuff for his catalogue of the damned: *I shall have to accept, myself, that gelatinous substance has often fallen from the sky – or that, far up, or far away, the whole sky is gelatinous? That meteors tear through and detach fragments? That fragments are brought down by stars?*

You should be in the geology section, then, she said, they've got a lovely collection of meteors there. We'll try the birds first, I think, he said; I'm really not that inclined to the cosmic.

Now abstracted, in no hurry, he roams up and down past cases of stuffed animals all stageily doing their thing: fox-cubs tumbling, otters on their hind legs looking surprised, rodents with perfect untrembling whiskers, and the huge suspended sea-turtle in its own special booth, telling its life story on a loop to all comers in a voice that sounds suspiciously like that of Richard Burton. At last, a heron.

11

He stands looking at it for a long while, unconsciously mimicking its stance, the pair of them equally thoughtful. It is you, isn't it? Has to be. Who else? Not the blessed coddymoddies, for sure, because they don't eat frogs and then regurgitate frog-associated by-products in a gelatinous mess. A mess which emphatically does not, Mr Fort, fall to earth in the wake of meteors from vast floating beds in the sky. Any more than frogs themselves do, in the normal course of things. Not that you're interested in the normal course of things, I know.

> *Two peculiarities of the fall of frogs:*
> *That never has a fall of tadpoles been reported*
> *That never has a fall of full-grown frogs been reported*
> *Always frogs a few months old.*

He can see it might be hard for some people to resist a man who writes nonsense with the authority of liturgy. He stands on the white steps now and blinks at the sun. Then he crosses the little park and waits for four lanes of traffic to stop and part and let him through. For a few long seconds as he crosses the road he has the sensation of walking in a riverbed filled to the brim with complete silence.

5.

In the rain it is often the stuffed animals, the wondrous talking turtle, Mam's stars. But today is bright and almost warm and so it is a walk in the park, a walk in the park, an absolute walk, he thinks, in the park. More metaphorical than real of course. Oh, he remembers walking, properly walking, hard and fast and with long strides across this same park to get to her room, and then back to his bedsit, drunk, in the dark, even when the park was chained and bolted against him, he knew the ways in and out.

This is not walking. There is no word to describe this amazing lack of forward progress across the face of the earth. It is hardly aimless, because nothing could be more intent, more determined. It is something like the way beetles move about, desperately busy but profoundly inexplicable, unless you know about beetles, or are one, when it must all make more sense. It is all directions and no direction. It gets us precisely nowhere. It puts that coffee, which would be ten or fifteen minutes away in real time, into the league of impossible tasks, up there with golden apples, the scissors-and-comb thing, and the sodding grail. Oh child, oh beetle, I should not have thought of the coffee. Now I am not an amused and nonchalant god. I am a strategic one, a cunning one; a god with ulterior motives. Come on little beetle, run this way! Catch me, if you can.

Teddy starts after Dan with a radiant grin, following the path like a charm, pulled in the wake of the rolling buggy. And yet when Dan turns round for the second time to shout encouragement the child appears to be miles back, sitting on the warm tarmac, tugging patiently at his shoe. Dan turns back on his tracks, bracing himself for the unequivocal refusal to be strapped back in. I am a bear, he says, by way of explanation, and he scoops the boy up with a growl and stuffs him into the buggy. It almost works. He fumbles the bloody straps, giving Teddy just enough time to realise that he is being cheated of his liberty, and summon his rage. It is not, Dan decides, even worth opening negotiations, and so he makes diagonally for the gate, head down, pushing hard, ignoring the sideways eyes of two elderly walkers. The pitch rises, the cries are louder and louder. Dan slows near the gate to let a woman through and then pushes the pram up onto the pavement where the child's sustained yell cuts out so suddenly his heart cramps in terror. He jams down the brake and bends over to see Teddy's raging face still furious, screaming in utter silence.

In seconds he has yanked off the harness, pulled the child into his arms and dragged the buggy back against the park railings onto the grass verge. The yell returns, full-blooded, uninterrupted. And then, as Teddy realises he is free again, subsides. They look at each other baffled. Shaking, Dan tucks his son tightly into him and negotiates the empty buggy with the other hand through the traffic and towards town.

6.

She calculates the time left against the tasks still to do. She will not finish them today, in half an hour; not in three hours; not in three days. She saves a file of work to do after supper, and then chooses three emails, and answers them carefully, conscientiously, ignoring the rising push of the rest like a reservoir filling, the authors full of excuses renegotiating deadlines in bad faith, the useless man from publicity, the requests that should have gone to a different department, and the upbeat, poisonous flow of criticism disguised as praise from the senior colleague. Smiley emoticons; tiny, barely perceptible barbs.

At twenty-five past she presses send for the third time, shuts down, straightens the piles on her desk and picks up her bag, her jacket, and goes into the toilets to do her hair and gloss her lips. Nods goodbye to the others, chats briefly on the stairs to the new girl and joins the scattering of people like her, spilling out of their offices. Many head for their cars, but she will walk home, looping in a daily twenty-minute detour to pass the building after it has closed, to have it emptied of its public, calm and stern. It should be more daunting this way, more focused on her, but oddly enough when there is no chance of going in she can often get closer, walking past it slowly. Twice she has found herself courageous enough to sit on the steps and listen to it breathing. On a bright spring afternoon that might, perhaps, feel possible.

She sets off briskly, clacking the heels of her new shoes. You really like those shoes, don't you? the senior colleague had said, and she had not known what to reply. Through the leafy car park, across the wide main road and through a scrap of building-site to the railway bridge. Where she lingers, because it is a busy time for trains and she knows one will be along soon. It turns the corner, endearingly short, a single carriage, like a determined grub. The squeal of the brakes and gears is pleasing; she waits for the rattle and rush of it on the long straight. But as she moves to the centre of the graffitied metal bridge to watch it approach the noise cuts out with the abruptness of a mute button, and the train passes under her in total, baffling silence.

7.

People Who Sit On Benches would, he thinks, make a great project. He must bring it up at their next strategy meeting.

So great, in fact, he would like to keep it for himself; work it into his ongoing Famous Footsteps project, there must be all kinds of exciting intersections there. Though getting much, indeed, any, historical depth on People Who Sit On Benches could be tricky, unless his Authors made something of them in their texts. How long have municipal benches been around in this country, he wonders. I mean, there's your starting point at least. No, maybe not. But an interesting joint project nevertheless, something performative, that could work pretty nicely. He will bring it up with the professor over a coffee first: test the water, stake a claim. He must make it clear whose brainchild this one is.

He walks on past the black guy as he has done fifty times before, but now feeling seriously self-conscious. It is a notebook day, he observes without quite looking. In spite of the drizzle. Not a cutting-up-university-prospectuses day. They must be stashed in the plastic bags. He almost has qualms: would a project like this mean talking to them? His normal subjects are literary and historical, that is to say, dead; he is not trained up for folklore, not folklore, what do they call it here, ethnography, talking to people. Perhaps they could get one of the postgrads to do that bit? The man doesn't look up as he goes past, but he is mumbling something. Luke quickens his pace and heads on up towards the campus. Remembers suddenly the curious new data problem with his maps. Something else to show the professor.

8.

The hospital appointment is awkwardly timed for late morning, so Myra has had to take a half-day. Tight and anxious, having slept very badly, she had left the flat far earlier than she needed to and walked into the centre, where she stood in a daze in various just-opening clothes shops, hoping for distraction. Bought nothing. Had an expensive coffee and a biscuit which she left untouched and read the letter again, Dear Ms Jones, your appointment with the consultant has been arranged for / *Annwyl Ms Jones, trefnwyd eich apwyntiad gyda'r ymgynghorydd*. Felt unenlightened in either language; knew that she missed her mum. Now she sits with her handbag tucked instinctively into her abdomen, pushing it gently against the pain. She has always associated this pain – mostly, during the day, a dull and perfectly manageable pain – with her fear of the colleague at work. Her GP has started to think otherwise.

She finds she has crossed the main road and the pocket of park in the light cold drizzle, past the beds of green shoots she hopes will become chocolate-black tulips again. There is a man on her bench. He is buttressed by old plastic bags full of magazines and papers. He is intently writing, sheltering his notebook with one hand; his lips move. She recognises him from somewhere. Another bench, she thinks, another part of town. It doesn't matter anyway because today she has no time to sit down and is in no mood to play games with the building; she does not feel proud or coy. She just needs it to look at her, give her a bit of its strength. So she carries on past the guy on her bench, past the little girl in bronze, and stands facing it, brave and vulnerable, her hands in the pockets of her raincoat.

Nothing happens.

She waits, looking directly at the main entrance, the pillars, the white steps, all the way up to the roof with its stately, allegorical figures and their absurd tufts of buddleia. The space where there ought to be a dragon. Two or three people come in and out, it is early, mid-week, not busy.

Still nothing.

There is not much time; soon she will have to catch her bus. She crosses the slip road and stands on the bottom steps, something she hasn't been able to do in a long time. And there, on the lower white steps, in the drizzle, as close as she dares, she feels a kind of panic rising; and nothing happens.

He takes the steps in his long stride two at a time and even he, deep in cogitation and looking forward to his meeting, feels her distress glance off him as he passes on his way up. Her image imprints on his mind between the bottom and the top step in a photographic flash. A white face, scared eyes, a mass of dark-red hair; a small figure in a tightly belted black mac, hands in her pockets. Unexpectedly, by instinct, he turns at the entrance to the building and calls down to her: Are you alright? Do you need any help? But she is facing the town now and it seems she cannot hear him: he has the profoundly dislocating sensation of having spoken and made no noise. He calls again, uselessly, into the wall of silence. He is on the verge of going back down to her when she gives a kind of shudder and stumbles down off the lower step and hurries across the park. He watches her go, then turns in through the big entrance where the sounds of voices seem suddenly magnified and restored, and heads for the woman at the desk, who recognises him, and smiles.

9.

Theo wasn't sure what he'd expected, but 'inconclusive' was not it. How, he wondered, in this precise and forensic day and age, could they not analyse and properly explain something so obviously biological? A rush of irritation came over him like a hot breath. He understood then that he was annoyed not so much with the people downstairs, although he had been mildly disappointed not to find the woman with the grey ponytail again, but with Charles Fort, no doubt thrilled to the tips of his spectral being in whatever astral plane he currently inhabits, crowing at this triumph of the Inexplicable over Science, a whole enlightened century on. They've sent it for further tests, is all, Mr Fort: we'll have rescued my star-rot from your host of the damned in another fortnight. Patience. Heron vomit, not the trailing mess of meteors, you'll see.

He grins, though, to find that he has drifted into Geology. He goes looking for the section on meteorites, if simply to face them down. Grey chips of stony meteorites; shiny slices of iron meteorites, and a curious hybrid of the two, a flat polished piece of metal full of small translucent chips, like pieces of yellow amber, as deliberately, teasingly aesthetic as any piece of modern sculpture. Left-overs, says the label almost casually, from the Primitive Material, from the origins; at least 4550 million years old. Before my time, replies Theo firmly, and turns to go.

A young father holds a small boy up against the glass nearby, an exhibit explaining the formation of stars. The child looks very young for such matters, almost a baby, but the father seems intent on quietly talking him through the whole thing before kissing his small blond head and setting him carefully down. Passing as the man straightens up Theo sees with a shock that there are tears in his eyes and for the second time that afternoon feels winded by someone else's distress. He pulls away quickly and makes for the main door. He will get the earlier train back. There might be an hour of daylight for the pond before he goes back to his mother, puts the bins out, cooks her supper, listens to her day.

10.

Thank you, says the professor, as Luke sits down with his face a little too red and his heart racing. Thank you very much for that, Luke. Now. How do the rest of us feel about this one?

There is some quiet nodding, a bit of supportive murmuring. Phoebe says brightly that she thinks it is a super idea with lots of potential. More nodding. Luke waits. Then gradually, gently, the resistance gets underway; constructive and thoughtful, they raise points of concern. There are ethical issues, of course. And questions of demarcation, as ever. Luke modestly raises his own concerns; historical depth; the difficulty of intersecting with the FF project. But mostly, it seems, they are worried about the name.

People Who Sit On Benches. I mean, would you be thinking PwSoB? Or PSB? It doesn't really...

Doesn't really *grab*.

And (this from the usual quarters): how are you thinking it will work in Welsh?

I hadn't got that far at this stage, says Luke hurriedly, it's early days.

Pobl sy'n Eistedd ar Feinciau, said Aslan. PEF. Or PsEaF, I suppose. *Be ti'n feddwl, Leusa?*

Dim rili yn ... t'wbod. Dim rili yn gweithio... Dim imi, ta beth. Sori.

Do you say *bainc* or *mainc*? says somebody. I never know which to use.

Either, says Aslan.

Sitters on Benches would be SOB, says somebody else. That has interesting connotations that could work.

A bit obvious? And maybe not always true?

PSOB would be more, um, playful.

Yes, that's not bad, I quite like that. PSOB.

The professor sits quietly, his head bowed, tapping the whiteboard marker in a subtle rhythm on his jeans and thinking not for the first time of a huge beach at low tide, acres of flat sand with ripple marks, and channels cutting through it with little rivulets branching off them, reaching outwards like veins, draining the water, sucking it down and away. Dissipation. The channels never made it to the sea. He waits two more minutes and then stands up and goes over to the whiteboard and writes:

BenchMarks / MeincNodiadau

There is a collective exhalation.

Three months, says the professor; you can have Phoebe, if you're happy with that, Phoebe? I can see interesting performative angles to this one. Put *Footsteps* on the back burner. Explore Income Flow from the Council – benches are quite their thing – check the ethical side with Social Services; Sioned can you help him with that? And maybe get the Samaritans lined up for Emotional Outreach. See how you get on. If we still like it in three months' time we can go large, contact Marketing, and see about rolling it out. Congratulations, Luke, it's a nice one.

Luke bows his head; inside it, a younger version of himself punches the air.

And now, says the professor, we had better get back to those ontological issues with Mapping the Unmappable. Aslan is going to talk us through it. Though I think, and he grins his disarming grin at them all, that we might be needing coffee and biscuits for this one.

11.

They had kept her waiting, which was as she expected. She tried to read the book she had chosen the night before but in the first waiting room there was a woman sobbing. The second waiting room was not a room but a row of four hard grey chairs against the wall of a corridor where she read a poster about lung cancer over and over again and watched people walk up and down. The third room was pink and involved less waiting. By then she had long over-run her half-day and phoned work to say she would not make it in at all. The secretary was away, and she had got the senior colleague who asked with great concern if she was ill. She had not known what to say.

The consultants had all been men. One had been kind. One did not exchange a single word beyond confirming her name and her age and asking if she might be pregnant; he did the rest from her notes. She lay very still and mute on the bed as he inserted the device and scanned her ovaries, talking in staccato to the nurse. Afterwards he turned back to his notes and the nurse had pulled a curtain, pointlessly, and helped her back into her underwear, her laddered tights. She had wept then, in humiliation and fear. Why didn't he talk to me? she said, suddenly fierce, and the nurse had looked surprised at the question. I'm sorry, she said. Not you, said Myra. Not you. Him.

More waiting then, ending with the kind consultant who said it was all still inconclusive but that unless something showed up on the scan they would wait for this lot of tests to come through, about a fortnight to three weeks, and they could talk about what to do then, plan the next stage. In the meantime he said to keep taking ibuprofen for the pain and deal with the bleeding as best she could. It might well sort itself out, he said, you never know.

The air at the bus stop is cold and wet and she is glad of it against her face, it makes her feel as if she really does exist. It is nearly four, and the day seems exhausted. She thinks then of the building wrapped in silence and decides she is not strong enough to risk any more humiliation. She changes buses in the centre of town, and goes home to her flat. There she has a hot bath, takes ibuprofen; deals with the bleeding as best she can.

12.

He feels his way out of the room in the dark. It is not possible to sleep with the child wheezing and coughing in bed beside him. Teddy is asleep, but barely; he is restless, close to breaking the surface, full of a cold that blocks his breathing, sends the air whistling round his chest. Dan has brought him into the big bed, worn out getting up to bend over the cot in the back room, hoping they can both settle, but it hasn't helped, and he has been lying there worrying about the money and the house, and knows now that he will not, cannot, sleep.

So he leaves the boy sprawled across most of the bed and sits in the kitchen wrapped in an overcoat, drinking beer. The house is cold and all his clothes are upstairs. He lets the sadness seep back into his tired body, it is too much to hold off in the dark, and when he knows there will be no stopping it he finds the Rainer cd and puts it on. Gets another beer, lets the song do its worst and puts his poor head down on folded arms and cries.

Where we are   is among the stars

The reason the house is cold is because it is suddenly colder outside. Cold enough to stop blossom, to spread an ice-film over grass. He knows that the night is clear and the air is sharp and northerly. And that even here in this city, inside the orange fug, the sky is laid bare and there are stars, her stars.

So many ways   that we   don't die.

When the sobs let go of him he finishes the beer and washes his face in cold water. Then he opens the kitchen door and stands with bare feet out in the yard, looking up into the space left him by variously angled roof-lines and the neighbour's holly. It is not enough. And before he knows what he has done he has pulled the bolt on the back gate and is out in the alley, hands deep in his pockets, cold feet heading for the park. The gates are locked but he knows the old ways through, and can still push between twisted railings into iced mud and undergrowth. He knows exactly where he is and should know how to find the path, except that it is pitch black and he stumbles around for a while with scrubby trees scratching his hands and face before breaking out onto the tarmac. He is making for the wide-open bit with the day-time view of the northern hills; the sky will be big enough there. He walks hard and fast, head down, the big Oxfam coat wrapped round his t-shirt and boxers; and wonders if there are others like him, or not like him, elsewhere in the huge park.

Leaving the path he strikes out across grass, wet and cold underfoot, the sky expanding above him until it is enough. Then he stands beneath it, neck craned, turning slowly to take his bearings and find Jane's patch of sky, her office, her place of work, the place that now absorbs her totally. A concentration of faded light. Stars dissolve if you look at them directly; he knows, because she taught him in this very place, the trick, the way of half-looking that captures their fugitive presence.

But into his head slinks the wolf. A dark grey shape slipping through a back gate swung open, nosing at a kitchen door barely ajar, heading for the stairs. All the stardust in the universe cannot stop the panic that now sends Dan running through the park with cold air tearing his lungs, towards the trees and the icy mud and the bent railings; down the back lane and into the yard where he bolts the gate and slams the door and storms up to the bedroom, where Teddy is deeply and comfortably asleep on his back, his arms thrown out as if in flight, breathing beautifully. Dan drops his coat on the floor and, covered in mud, climbs in and wraps himself shivering around his son. His raw feet thaw into a grateful pain.

13.

A sorry mess of dead frogspawn. Translucence clouded, like the eye of a fish filming over, whiteish-grey. A week ago he had rejoiced to see the sudden clumps of jelly, that first sighting always unexpected, however much he expects it. Blighted by the sharp breath of this frost: the waste, he thinks, not for the first time, though he knows there is still hope for more. A fragile coat of ice across most of the pond. He walks round it once, checking for signs of life noted two days ago, but things are holding back again now, like the waiting buds, the creatures have slowed right down. It will come in a terrible rush when it comes, he thinks, and runs over possible permutations for the different species, the effects of the delay on their patterns of growth, their chances of breeding, of survival. It wasn't always bad. There would be surprises as a consequence of this cold.

And it means he can still plant trees. And planting a tree this morning, ahead of all the tasks that lie waiting, would be a good thing, a way of quelling the nag of anxiety, his apprehension that everything is about to be disrupted. It is a feeling he hates worse than disruption itself. A small sturdy upright tree would somehow offset the fall. He strikes out across the field towards the nursery. Damson. Hazel? No, damson. She loves the jam. And she can still be pretty sharp, herself. He wishes she hadn't called him by his dead brother's name. The first time, he thinks, that she has ever done that.

As the spade pushes into the hard ground he reorganises the day in his head. He'd had to cancel the school session, because of visiting times and trains; but he could move the contract work forward by an hour and a half. He'd have an extra hour on the train – no, two, there and back – for the paperwork. Though he knows that on the journey back he will be more likely to read or look out of the window. He gets down on his knees, and his big hands gently, gradually, release the tangle of roots from the compacted earth.

14.

In spite of herself Myra is on her bench. Shivering. And still ignored. I am going back to the hospital, she thinks quietly, and I would appreciate a flicker of concern, a little kindness. She is irritated with herself for coming back at all. You said you'd go shopping, buy a nice cardigan, some new wool for a scarf, you said you wouldn't come up this far today, you could have arranged lunch with Elin, you have only yourself to blame. But work was painful: the senior colleague has started bringing her cake. Handing it over publicly, as if to an invalid, saying how frail she looks, how pale she looks, how she must build herself up. Myra, who has no objection to cake in the normal course of things, could not eat a mouthful. She took it home, left it in the tin until it blossomed with mould, then threw it out and put the tin through the dishwasher till it shone, returned it with thanks, and waited with a kind of low-level dread for the next one. It all added to her anxiety, the thought of the waste; she felt she should distribute it among the poor or something, but didn't know how.

She looks up to find a man standing in front of her. He has a plump, earnest face and is holding an iPad.

Ah, hello, he says; softly American.

She looks just past him, to the left of his ear, disapprovingly.

I'm sorry to interrupt …

His embarrassment is terrible but Myra is not inclined to help. He takes a deep breath.

My name is Dr Luke Stringer, I work at the University, in the Department of Cultural Cartography. I'm leading a research project. On people. Who, ah, people who sit. On Benches.

For a fraction of a second she looks as if this might be funny, but then reverts to flickering disapproval.

Luke is in agonies. He told them he would be no good at this. He is an Ideas Man. She was the only one he had agreed to interview, the one who had appeared on paper the least threatening, the most normal, an office girl on a lunch-break with a fondness for a particular place. He summons his nerve, and the words come all in a rush.

Look, he says. I'm really sorry. Please just let me show you quickly and then I'll leave you in peace. I'm not trying to sell anything or get you involved in anything, it's just that we need a few stats for the mapping programme and it would be really helpful … just a few questions … nothing personal. May I show you? May I, ah, sit down?

His small deft fingers swish and tap the screen, pulling up an intricate logo with the words *BenchMarks/MeincNodiadau* wrapped dynamically around a stylised park bench. He taps on the image of the bench and reaches a series of questions, which he waves in front of her. Look, he says. It's not that much really, and of course you don't have to answer them all. Or, he adds helplessly, any of them. Of course. May I?

It is, thinks Myra, better than battling with an uncooperative building. She nods her head very slightly and moves up the bench to make room for him, holding her bag tightly on her lap.

Ok, here goes. Ah, name? Optional, of course. Miss?

Jones, says Myra, unexpectedly.

Marvellous, said Luke. That's marvellous. Miss Jones. Ah, OK, age range? He shows her the categories. Optional also, of course.

She glances sideways at the screen. 30-35, she said.

Marvellous. Thank you. Profession?

Copy-editor.

Interesting. And, ah, how often do you come to sit on this particular bench? More than three times a week; once-a-week; once-a-fortnight; once-a-month. Less; more?

Once a week, says Myra firmly. If that. Less.

OK, thank you, says Luke, who knows that is nonsense. She wouldn't have shown up on their Scoping Exercise if her visits were that infrequent. They were starting with the heavy-use subjects, after all. It occurs to him to wonder, with a slightly sinking heart, if she really is called Jones. But he soldiers on.

And ah, finally, if you don't mind me asking that is, Miss Jones, ah, why do you come to sit on this particular bench?

To eat my lunch, says Myra.

Marvellous, thank you. And, ah, do you have any other favourite benches in the city?

No, says Myra.

Well, thank you, Miss. I'll leave you in peace now, if you could just sign this form here to say that you don't mind us using your answers in our database and maps?

She thinks about this for a few seconds, then leans over and scribbles on the paper.

How does it become a map? she asks.

The data is geo-referenced, he says.

It becomes a map of benches?

Mm. And of the connections between them, the ah, pathways people take through the city to get to them. Oh yes: where is your office again?

He looks around vaguely.

Just over there, says Myra, gesturing towards town.

OK. Well the benches are like nodes, he says. I've got a prototype here, look, I'll show you.

It looks like a net or a web, but with no symmetry. Random thin black lines criss-crossing, heading in and out of the dark spots she assumes are the benches.

It doesn't look like anywhere, she says. How do you know where they are?

He taps, and there is a ghostly background, a map of the centre with the park and the river, the castle, all the civic buildings, her building.

You can change what happens in the background by playing with the data, he says. He makes it turn blue and green.

I quite like the pure one, the empty one, she says. Show me again.

The lines reach out in delicate curves between the nodes. Like molecules in a chemistry text book, she thinks. Or those maps you get of constellations, that look nothing like their names.

Why are some of them broken? she asks.

There were tiny hairline cracks in several threads, white lines, as if a child had taken one of those disappearing-ink pens and scribbled over the top. Luke flushes. It's a software problem, he says. They're not supposed to do that. We're working on it right now.

She fishes in her bag for her phone and checks the time. I have to go back to work, she says.

Of course, says Luke, getting up and dropping his piece of paper, getting flustered as he picks it up. Thanks again for your time.

Good luck with your project, she says. And then, as she was about to go, remembers the black guy with the plastic bags. Does anyone else use this bench regularly?

Ah, I'm not sure, says Luke, suddenly unable to remember what the policy is on sharing data directly with subjects. But I can let you know.

15.

The bus is packed. He has an aisle seat towards the back and has been obliged to fold his long legs into his body as the people standing force themselves further and further in. Mostly students; he can see no one who seems to need his seat more than he does, and sinks deep into his mind to escape. He thinks of his trees in bud. Then of the tiny fish he believes are circling deep in the centre of the pond, of the promise of the first flash of a sighting once this bitter March cold breaks. Of the heron he had surprised early one morning in the reed-bed, peering inscrutably into grey water. Probably stuffed with frogspawn, he thought; they have it coming every which way this year, poor frogs. The bus rolls and judders at the lights. People shoulder their way apologetically on and off. Of the brave damson newly planted, shocked, but gathering strength.

And then he looks up astonished into the pale face of the woman with the dark red hair, falling towards him in the surge. He gets to his feet entirely without thinking and, with a hand on her shoulder, pushes her gently down into his seat.

Thank you, says Myra, equally surprised.

Not at all, says Theo courteously, and moves backwards into a standing space, looking firmly out through the window on the other side, as if afraid she might feel his gaze on the back of her neck.

Mayhem at the university stop, but then the bus is transformed. There are spaces between the passengers. They breathe out and settle and relax. Except for her. He watches her from where he is now sat near the back, stretching his long legs down the aisle. She has shunted up to the window and sits pressed against the glass, her bag pulled hard into her body.

He isn't surprised when she gets to her feet just before the hospital stop; he does the same, shadowing her almost protectively as she gives a little half-nod of thanks to the driver and steps down onto the pavement. She glances up at him as if she wholly expects him to be there, as if she finds it a comfort to see him, and then she slings her bag onto her shoulder and sets off briskly for the main entrance. He slows his natural pace right down and lets her go.

16.

Teddy is enjoying the steps. *Un dau, un dau; un dau.* He goes up on all fours but comes down dangerously upright, delighted with himself, and hasn't fallen yet. Dan is sitting halfway up the first flight, not quite reading, with half an eye and half an ear on his son and any passers-by who might trip over him. It is just April, the sun is back, and this time it feels as though spring might actually happen.

After a while he notices a tall, pale-haired man further along the steps who appears to be behaving in much the same way as Teddy. He takes the shallow steps extremely slowly, one at time, and keeps stopping. He looks almost as though he is listening. He might, though Dan can't quite tell, also be humming. He goes up and down, up and down, but only the higher flight nearest the entrance. Yes, he is humming. His behaviour makes Dan suddenly highly alert for the child; though he can't tell if this is genuine eccentricity or some kind of performance art. Either way it is disturbing. He moves along to be closer to Teddy, and considers taking him down to the patch of park where he can run in circles around the gorsedd stones and the flowerbeds. But Teddy is so happy with the steps, and the man, who seems vaguely familiar, is so wholly absorbed in moving slowly up and down, listening, that Dan soon gets used to the idea of them both, such very different sizes, doing much the same thing. He picks up his book again, starts wondering about lunch.

And then the tall man is not going up and down, he is moving, just as slowly, along a single step three or four down from the top, still with that same listening expression. And it happens that he is the nearest person to Teddy when he finally topples forward, *un dau, un dau...*

Tri, says Theo seriously, holding out a big hand to catch and steady him. He sets him back on his feet and then offers a finger, which Teddy grabs, and leads him down a step at a time to Dan, who is running up to meet them.

Thank you, says Dan, scooping Teddy up. Thanks.

Not at all, says Theo, recognising them from the meteors.

I knew he'd fall over in the end; he's not that steady coming down.

He's doing a great job, says Theo, when you think how little he is.

I should have kept a closer eye; he sort of drifted away.

Hard at this age, says Theo, reassuring him.

Teddy is wriggling to be free again and holds out his arms to Theo, a potential accomplice. Theo grins and gives him a hand.

Un dau tri, he says. And then, to Dan, do you want to see something very odd?

Dan shrugs noncommittally, he is still not sure. But he puts Teddy back down on the steps.

Look, says Theo, take his other hand and watch this. With the little boy between them they climb the top flight of shallow steps, one at a time, counting out loud in Welsh.

Un ... dau ... tri ... ped... Their voices cut out ... and then return ... *chwech, saith.* And they are standing at the top, under the portico, people pushing past them for the entrance, looking at each other over Teddy's head.

Down? says Theo. Dan nods.

Un ... dau ... tr-.............-war, pump, chwech, saith.

OK, says Dan. I see what you mean. I'm sorry, I thought you were, you know, a bit...

Of a nutter, agrees Theo comfortably. Well yes, but no more than most.

It's not just here, he adds. It happens in other places too.

Dan looks straight at him. I know, he says.

They sit down on the top step of the lower flight and Dan fishes a rice-cake out for Teddy. He tells Theo about the episode near the park gates, and Theo tells him of two other places he has come across in town. Though it shifts around a bit, he says, the silence doesn't always flow along quite the same lines.

And while they are talking a man comes and stands in front of them, holding an iPad, looking deeply concerned.

Dan! he says.

Dan looks at him blankly.

It is Dan James, isn't it? It's me, Luke. From the department. The seminars? Postgraduate seminars? Five ... six years ago? We did that mapping literature project together.

Light dawns slowly. Dan stands up and shakes his hand.

I heard, ah, about Jane, says Luke. I am sorry. Is this...?

Teddy, yes, says Dan. Thank you.

Theo gets up to go with a friendly nod to them both. I'll

see you around, he says. I'm just going inside.

Do you work here? says Luke, with sudden interest.

No, says Theo, I just visit.

Ah, says Luke, disappointed. It's just … I'm, ah, looking for someone. But maybe you come here quite often?

Not terribly often, says Theo. I don't live in town.

We do, says Dan. Who are you after?

A woman, says Luke. A woman with red hair who sits on that bench down there.

I know who you mean, says Dan. I've seen her.

Theo, who has already started back up the steps, turns sharply and looks down at them.

She's in hospital, he says. At least, about a week ago, I saw her go in.

17.

No cat no goldfish, she said, and closed her eyes. The nurse smiled and left. No lynx no bears no lions no monkeys. Not even an aardvark snuffling behind the sofa. The plants will die, though. She must remember to text Elin and ask her to take the little orange tree and anything else she likes. But how will she get the key to her?

Perhaps having a long break from the bench, from the truculent building, will do her good, she thinks. When she comes back in a week, maybe two, the velvet black tulips will be out and the building will be so glad to see her it will give her its complete attention, and she will know she was missed, and who can ask for more than that? But she must wait until she is quite well again, to get some life and strength back. She has no intention of being an object of pity.

When she wakes again she is uncomfortable and needs the loo. It is a short walk down the corridor, a million miles away. This is what old is like, she thinks. People everyday their hearts sinking at the million miles. Come on, Myra. She cannot wait for unpredictable nurses. She hates to ring for help. Slowly, slowly, she shifts her legs sideways off the bed, and at the same time pulls herself up into a sitting position. A peculiar movement, she thinks, in different directions, like being the arm of some complicated swing bridge. The sitting is painful, tugs at the wound in her abdomen. Then she slips gently down onto her bare feet and takes a deep breath. It is not so bad. Not so bad.

On the way back, however, she has to sit on a chair in the corridor for a minute to get her strength back. She composes her face into an expression of impregnable cheer, so that no one will dare to ask if she is all right. No one comes past to ask. She closes her eyes and breathes in and out. Then stands up far too quickly, and before she can do a thing about it there is a rush of darkness closing around her vision and she is keeling forward into white space. The hands that catch her and guide her firmly back to her chair are not those of a nurse.

Thank you, says Myra, too dazed to be properly surprised.

Not at all, says Theo, gently. This time he sits down beside her. She waits for him to ask if she is all right, but he doesn't.

I got up too fast, she says.

Yes.

I'll be ok now, I think.

Give it a minute, he says. And then adds, you know you look quite odd without your raincoat.

I'll try to remember it next time I need the loo.

You do that, he says.

Why, she says, are you wandering the corridors of the women's ward?

My mother fell and broke her leg a few days ago. She's further down in the next section. I'm going to visit her now.

Oh. Is she doing ok?

I don't know, he says. They say she is, but she's not herself. I don't much like it.

Oh. Myra looks concerned. Look, I'm fine now. Thank you for catching me.

Again, he says.

She pulls a wry face. Yes. Sorry. I'll try to keep my balance a bit better next time.

Come on, he says, getting up. Come on, let me see you back. Is it this way?

And he gives her his arm with such eighteenth-century politeness that she laughs, and forgets to bristle, and is glad of the support. He hands her carefully back to her bed and gives a little nod.

Don't go gallivanting around too much, will you?

I will try to restrain myself, she says.

18.

There are seven screens in his office, and a different map on every one. The colours are lovely. The professor walks round and round, stopping for a few seconds in front of each, until he finally sits down at the largest console. He clicks a few times, pulling the maps in one on top of the next so that they form a palimpsest, like layers of tracing paper, he hasn't seen tracing paper in years, he wonders if it still exists, if people still use it; it was never, he thinks, quite translucent enough. He selects seven more maps, then seven more, thickening the layers on the big screen.

In any case, here is confirmation. The blankness eating through the fine lines of every map is itself a pattern, a new map – one which does not correspond to any of his. The invisible lines, though not quite a perfect match in every layer, form a tracery of nothingness. Strands of it, reaching out like veins and arteries across the city, with tendrils twisting and curling off the main stems. All of them flowing out of what appears to be a pool of emptiness in the middle of the castle.

It is, he now knows this for certain, nothing to do with him or any of his team. He has thought of it till now as a virus, a poisonous piece of software with a life of its own; a slow malicious joke, perhaps, against the new regime by one of those ousted when the changes came a few years back. But words have been coming back to him from the streets, his project-workers dropping by in ones and twos, quietly baffled, all unsettled, handing over their worm-eaten data and talking uncomfortably of gaps and walls and sudden silences. And he has been out and found them for himself; has listened attentively to the quality of the nothingness. And, though it is in many respects a setback for the project as a whole, he must admit that he has been secretly pleased to find his maps, his data-tools, his programmes sensitive enough to pick up something so unplanned-for, so utterly impossible to predict.

He will have to get into the castle, it appears. This has not been particularly easy since ButeCo kindly took it back off the City during the last economic crisis. He remembers going as a child, with his brother, the two of them running in mad circles on the grass and urging their mother to take them up the keep, though she said it made her dizzy, horribly dizzy, they were pitiless and made her climb up after them. Scampering feet spiralling up ahead of her; he thinks of her now holding on to the curve of the rail and forcing her own feet to follow, one step after the other, her desperate anxiety for them chasing on ahead of her, like a hawk after sparrows, oblivious little sparrows, who never felt the rush of her panic, and never, ever stopped. The keep is gone now though, of course. It must look empty in there.

He knows enough of the right people, he thinks. He will find a way in. But the chance must not be wasted. This stuff, this silence, must be properly analysed. And as he stands there in the centre of his office an idea grows inside him as quickly and irresistibly as a smile, and sets his pulse beating, and has his slim fingers reaching for his phone, and scrolling through the names to find an old, old number.

19.

Teddy is asleep in the pushchair, with his rabbit wedged under a cheek to keep his head more or less propped up.

He is as flushed as a real live cherub, and is drooling onto the rabbit's matted fur. One small hand grasps a wooden tractor in a grip of steel.

So, after you, ah, finished the PhD...

We were in the States for year, a bit more. Jane was in the second year of her research post at NASSR, and then we were expecting him, and then they found the tumour, so we came back here to be near her parents and she had the baby and died three months later.

Luke looks into the swirls of his coffee, and then at the sleeping child.

He's very beautiful.

Yes. Yes, he is.

They drink their coffee in silence for a while, then Luke asks, Have you tried to do anything with your thesis?

You mean publish?

Mmm.

No, no time to think. I'm too tired. And I'm not sure I could now. I don't even read much any more. Except to him.

Luke thinks about this. I'm not sure I actually read that much any more either, he says. I mean I work with literary texts from dawn to dusk, but it's mostly, ah, sort of ingesting them through various programmes and doing stuff with the data.

The maps, you mean? Like the one you showed me, with the benches.

Yes, though the first ones were more, ah, literary, based on texts. I actually started off just helping out with data-input on the *Ulysses* project; that was ten years ago and as far as I know it's still going.

I remember that one, says Dan happily. Epic.

Quite. Then it got to be more about where writers were when they did their writing, and I co-managed a project on the BL in the 1920s, lots of famous footfalls there as you can imagine, it was very pretty to map, all radiating outwards.

Woolf, says Dan.

Yep. Lovely following her. And Fort, he was very neat to plot, very predictable, in and out at regular times and never really straying outside his square mile even after work.

Fort?

Charles, you know: the anomalies man, collector of the weird and wonderful. *Book of the Damned*. Though he'd actually published that by the time he came over. Did the same sort of stuff in London, though.

Don't think I've read him.

You should, he's very big on stars.

Then what?

Then it was another London one called 'And Did Those Feet?' says Luke.

And Did They?

Mostly, yes.

Whose?

Weird religious sects of the 1790s. Swedenborgians; Southcottians, followers of Richard Brothers, those types.

You get around a bit, then, if it's Cardiff park benches now.

Sort of a sideline, this one, says Luke. And then, thoughtfully scraping the froth out of the bottom of his cup, I hope that woman, that Miss Jones with the red hair, I hope she's going to be OK.

Theo will tell us, says Dan. Teddy begins to stir.

20.

The word knitting, he thinks, does not even begin to capture it. Knitting is thick and warm and heavy, the tank-tops and sweaters they used to wear on the farm. Tea-cosies, bobblehats; the two largely indistinguishable. But what tumbled from her needles over the hospital sheets was like mist, like breath itself, all silver and light, a pale grey silk that curled and twisted inwards. From a distance she could have been knitting a waterfall. Who is it for, he had said, in quiet amazement, and she had shrugged and smiled.

Now he walks from room to room in his mother's house, collecting fresh clothes, a book, an old photo of his dad. She – they – have been in for ten days or more, and all of time seems to have altered as a result. He wonders, now, thinking about it, if knitting was something his mother ever did, or might do. He has no recollection of seeing her with a pair of needles. Perhaps a bit late to start now. But he comes across her drawing things, the charcoals, a sketchbook, and the little pocket watercolours. Everything goes into a big hessian bag, where it looks hopelessly eclectic. If he had been a girl, he thinks pointlessly; then, if there had at least been a daughter-in-law, she would have known what was appropriate. The various nearly-daughters-in-law flit briefly before him, but they all look decidedly unhelpful.

In her bedroom he stoops over the dressing table and peers at his curious face reflected in triplicate, and then continually inwards, or possibly outwards, and an odd-looking face it is from any angle. He wonders if there is a necklace or a ring that might please her, and dips his huge hands, burglar's hands, into the carved wooden box. Pearls: Scottish river pearls, he bought her those; a string of tiny jet beads with bevelled edges. He chooses an amethyst brooch that belonged to his gran, and a small silver pendant he clearly remembers her wearing when they were children. Then his fingers find something he doesn't recognise, a bracelet, very simple; three strands of silver intertwined. He will ask her about it, see if she can remember a story.

He works hard down at the pond in mild drizzle all afternoon. A spiderweb hanging off the rushes recalls Myra's silver thread. The second time he had passed her part of the ward the curtains had been drawn. But two days later she had been there, propped up, knitting, and looked not unpleased to see him. She should have been allowed out by now, she said, at any rate for a few days after the biopsy, but the problem was that she fainted every time she stood up. Absurdly low blood pressure, she said; my heartbeats are too far apart, or something.

You look a bit, well – translucent, he said critically. As if you might be gradually vanishing. Are you eating properly?

I eat what they give me, mostly, she said; though that's hardly properly.

So he had offered, of course.

Well, she said, if you are passing M&S. Where do you live, anyway?

Out, he said. An hour away. Tell me what you'd like.

The really posh fruit salad, she said, the one with pomegranate seeds and blueberries and mango and, well, everything. And Greek yoghurt – the thickest, the really creamy kind –

Anything else? His eyebrows were quizzical.

And some... She caught his tone just too late and shut

her mouth and shook her head. Then looked at him sideways, and added, very quickly … and freshly squeezed lemonade and the seed mix, the stuff that looks like superdeluxe birdfood.

He laughed. Mam wants a packet of Rich Tea biscuits.

It's a generation thing, said Myra crisply, and gave all her attention to her mercurial knitting.

As he headed out to the corridor she had called out softly: thank you. He grinned, pretended not to hear.

Now he is absorbed, skimming off bunches of duckweed and crowsfoot; fishing out beetles and larvae for the starter tanks, adding scoops of frogspawn, the tiny black commas just beginning to flick with life. He has six or seven tanks ready to go, but will have to wait for the others to come back with the van. And since three of the drop-offs are in the city he will do this run with them, and call in to the hospital again, and get an evening train back. The nurses like him, don't mind him coming at odd hours; and she needs a clean nightdress, and she will be pleased with the Rich Teas.

21.

The professor meets her at the station. She took some persuading. Seven days. The song goes round in his head, the

Dylan song, seven days. I'll be waiting at the station. *And she'll be comin' on forth... My beautiful comrade from the North*.

And she does. And she is, with her honeybrown hair all streaked with grey, and the crinkles round her laughing eyes, and though he does not catch her by the waist and swing her round, he hugs her hard, and then they stand back and look at each other for a full five seconds, and burst out laughing. He wins the tussle over her bag and they leave the station, still laughing. As he leads her up into town he reaches into his pocket for his phone and, one-handed, begins to text.

Hotel. Drop bag. Coffee?

She glances at her phone and smiles and texts him back.

Nice suit.

I know.

With the lightest touch to her arm he manoeuvres her across roads, threads them both through the busy arcades, glancing down and up, and at her bright face, as the words fly between their phones.

You read what I sent?

On the train.

Journey?

Bliss. Five hours to myself.

Kids OK?

Most of them, most of the time. Yours?

Long gone: doing her own thing. Not an academic, thank god.

Mine will become accountants.

And wear Nice Suits.

Somehow they make the hotel without serious collisions. He orders coffee and while she checks in and finds her room he collects his briefcase from behind the desk and sets up the screen with the map of the twisting blank tendrils, and picks over the sheaf of papers prepared for him by Luke. Because, he thinks, if anyone can grasp the quality and intent of this stuff it will be Meg Vaughan, Director of *Distaw Rhwydd/ Théâtre du Silence*, dancer, tight-rope walker, fierce theoretician of the performing arts, erstwhile bloody impossible colleague and so profoundly deaf and dumb since birth that she is acknowledged across the world as the servant, ambassador, and queen of silence.

She slips into the seat beside him, and places an iPad across the solid arm of the chair, and their hands play a quick duet of questions and answers and more questions, and her eyes meeting his are as sharp as they ever were. Come to bed, he thinks; but he knows they have very little time. The castle has agreed to open the gates at five, but only for half-an-hour, and he wants her to see some of the main channels through the city, the wall at the museum, and the swirls around Luke's benches. He shows her their itinerary, and though she mocks him for his flashy technology and his over-careful preparation he can see that she is as curious and excited as he is, every bit.

22.

There is a whiteness to the light, like being abroad. She cannot think why she has never walked this way before, it is lovely, a cycle-track and footpath with trees and primroses along a little river, coming out quite unexpectedly at the side of the Gorsedd gardens, where the road should be; she doesn't think to wonder what they've done with it. She has a new dress, soft, charcoal, with a simple neckline. Her white arms are scented lightly with suncream, a citrus tang; there are sunglasses pushed up high on her head, and her lips are dark-copper to match her hair. She goes click-clack on the path in her heels and then stops at the slip-road in sudden admiration at the building in the beautiful light, its pillars whiter, taller, more elegant than she has ever seen them. And for once the regard seems mutual, as if the building too has just caught its breath. She click-clacks up the shallow steps like a film star, one hand running up the smooth metal railings, and stands for a moment in front of the entrance, as it breathes its visitors in and out. And then she walks very deliberately to the alcove in the wall at the back, and first with one hand, and then the other, lays her palms flat against the smooth stone, and smiles. Then she puts her face to it, sideways, listening. And now she is pressed up against the wall with her whole body, listening, listening, because at long last after all that cruel silence the building has said to her come quickly, come now, there is something only you can hear, come and listen, it will happen very soon now. And so she is listening deep into the stone for that rare geological event, a heartbeat. Once in a million years, or thereabouts, depending on the type of stone of course, she can't remember the figures now, but even for Portland Stone dressed up as Parthenon Marble it is several hundred thousand and some, and decimal points, there are always decimal points, between one deep heart-beat and the next. With her eyes closed and the sun on the back of her neck and her milk-white self pressed flat against the building she waits, and listens, beyond the noise of the people on the steps and the patient rumble of school buses and the traffic beyond, and she has never been so beautiful in her whole life, so that the cold which follows is worse than unpleasant, worse than disappointment, worse than anything. It is a cold room, empty; darkened perhaps by blinds, and she is sitting on a plastic chair while someone walks around her, and around her. She is holding, in both hands, an incredible object made of glass, a spherical object with long, impossibly delicate spines, like a frozen star or a sea-urchin, or like skeins of pulled sugar, so crystalline and utterly fragile that she can only focus on holding it, on not breaking it, and cannot look up to see the face of the man, it is always a man, mocking her over and over as he walks around her and around, saying please do not touch, please do not touch, please... And it is cold because she is in her underwear and the circling is closer and closer, and the voice is slower and slower, please ... do ... not ... touch ... please ... do ... not ... and she knows that when the fingers finally brush across her shoulders and neck it will be like chalk scraping the blackboard, and she will clamp her teeth and clench her hands and there will be such a shattering of delicate glass and the voice is getting closer and slower and she cries out *please*, holding her glass object, *please do not touch, do not touch, please...*

And it is a hellish long time for everybody before another voice, gentle, urgent, finally breaks through to her from the other side, saying Myra, come back, no one will touch you, no one will hurt you Myra, wake up, come on, come back, it's me, I'm here, and look – I've got your fruit-salad.

23.

The benches are emptying. Dan and Teddy have started doing an unofficial round for Luke, now busy with the crisis team and enjoying every minute. The project has not been shelved, exactly, but the Interference, as they call it in the department, has had a significant effect on what they can do. A lot of time now goes on briefing the media and the ministers, and trying to squash the wilder speculations in the press. The benches database is on hold, at any rate, and it has become a question of managing things, of keeping an eye.

Luke buys them lunch or coffee every couple of days and they keep him informed. And Dan is grateful: for the food, because money is tight, and for the company, because his world is full of the mothers of young children, and he sees few men his own age. For the project itself, and the motivation it provides to get going, to plan routes, to fit the walking around playgroup and shopping; and of course, the sitters on the benches are drawing him in.

He talks more naturally to strangers than Luke ever could, and besides, Teddy is superb at breaking the ice. With every new round, as they move from a nod and a smile to a few words, they feel they are making friends. Teddy learns how to drop a scattering of coins in the hat of the vigorous guy singing Irish rebel songs; he learns not to try and scoop the contents of the hat out again. Dan tells Luke about the peculiar effect of leaning forward to drop the money and having the song cut out abruptly and then cut in again as you straighten up. Like a radio in a power cut. A blip. The black guy with the notebooks and the plastic bags chuckles with pleasure when he sees the child, and cuts him a tree, or a smiling face, or a bright logo, out of his university prospectuses. The Syrian lady saves them unsuitable boiled sweets. And apart from one lad with shocking pale blue eyes and (he guesses) a drug problem, who has never spoken and radiates a misery so intense that Dan cannot bring himself to stop, not with Teddy, they all, in their exchanges, seem glad to give him scraps of their lives.

I have a son, too, she says, *but he is grown-up, and far away.*

I'm from Leicester, says the busker. *When I was a kid I always wanted to be Irish.*

He doesn't pass much of this on, unless it's particularly funny, but just notes who, and where, and when; there's no room on the frozen database for all these back-stories. But he comes to see soon enough that he is not the only one lugging an ugly great loss around, that dull misshapen metallic lump. These meteor crashes, he thinks, what do they do to us, how do we manage. Extinction.

In the space of a fortnight these encounters are noticeably fewer. Over half the benches, as often as not, are empty; the sitters seem to come less often, and there are one or two people he hasn't seen at all, in spite of some bright days, some lovely days, when the whole business of sitting on a Cardiff bench might be something, he thinks, that you could do with complete and utter conviction.

24.

When he comes back twenty minutes later from sitting beside his sleeping mother Myra is propped up in bed with her fruit salad, picking out the pomegranate seeds and eating them thoughtfully, one at a time. There is a slightly disconcerting brightness about her eyes. The nurse brings them both tea.

He settles in the chair beside her bed; the same chair as the one beside his mother, he thinks; doing exactly the same job. You sit next to them and they are miles away. *Oh Myra what is the matter with you.* He would like to reach over and gently touch her face but understands that he must not touch her at all. So he nods, sideways.

Better?

Yes. She offers him the tub of fruit and his unwieldy fingers find a grape.

Good. He fishes in his bag for a book and pulls it out. Do you mind, he says, I mean is it OK if I sit here for a bit? My mother is fast asleep and my train isn't for a while.

She just smiles. He smiles back.

Do you read much? he says, gesturing pointlessly at his book.

No, she says. Never.

He raises his eyebrows.

It's what I do for a living, she says defensively. All day

long. Copy editing. Commas and capitals and the spaces in between. Why would I read at home?

Different kind of reading, he says sternly. Quite different. Why not?

Eyes, she says. They get tired. And I get tired; I don't need all those words.

So what do you do?

Radio, music. Cook. Telly sometimes. And knitting.

I thought you city folks hung out in bars the whole time, or the cinema, or the theatre.

Not me, she said. Not ever. What about you?

When I'm not at the pond, or working, or cooking for my mother, yes, I read.

What do you read?

He grins. Stuff about ponds, mostly.

And your work?

Ah, well, yes. That's ponds too.

Which is perfectly true, he thinks, so why does it suddenly seem so funny? Her eyes are bright with laughter.

No, really. We have a small company, a co-operative thing, *Corsydd Cymru/Welsh Wetlands*. We have a website and a logo and everything.

Conservation, she says, rolling it nicely on her tongue.

It's more proactive than that, he says.

She finishes the fruit and licks her fingers. Drinks her cold tea with a wrinkled nose. Then she settles back into her pillows and closes her eyes. He can't tell what kind of pain it is that flickers across her face. Her eyes open wide and stare at the ceiling.

I'm too frightened to go to sleep again.

If you would just let me hold your hand, he thinks. But says, instead: It won't happen again, not like that, it never does.

You'll sleep fine this time, it won't come back.

It might. I can feel it. Waiting.

Is it a dream you've had before?

She shudders. No, she says. I have bad dreams sometimes but this one is quite, quite new.

He should change the subject but can't. Is there any point, he says slowly, almost off-hand, holding his breath, is there any point talking? Exorcism...

No, she says swiftly. No. No. Her face closes down and she turns her head away from him.

Then I'll read to you, he says. This is Charles Fort. He's mad, but great to read out loud. Mam likes him a lot. 1904, this is. *The Book of the Damned*. He collects scientific anomalies; he especially likes things falling out of the sky:

I think of a region somewhere above this earth's surface in which gravitation is inoperative...

I think that things raised from this earth's surface to that region have been held there until shaken down by storms...

The Super-Sargasso Sea.

Derelicts, rubbish, old cargoes from interplanetary wrecks; things cast into what is called space by convulsions of other planets, things from the times of the Alexanders, Caesars and Napoleons of Mars and Jupiter and Neptune; things raised by this earth's cyclones: horses and barns and elephants and flies and dodoes, moas and pterodactyls; leaves from modern trees and leaves of the Carboniferous era – all, however, tending to disintegrate into homogenous-looking muds or dusts, red or black or yellow – fishes dried and hard, there a short time: others there long enough to putrefy...

She relaxes into it. Smiles at the elephants, and finally interrupts to ask why on earth he would be reading it? It is not, she says, even remotely about ponds.

Ah but you're wrong. There's quite a lot about ponds, ponds in space, falling out of the sky, it's how he explains all those falls of little frogs and live fish, listen to this:

We accept that there are bodies of water and also clear spaces – bottoms of ponds dropping out – very interesting ponds, having no earth at bottom...

That there is water – oceans or lakes or ponds, or rivers of it – that there is water away from, and yet not far-remote from, this earth's atmosphere and gravitation...

The pain of it:

A whole new science to learn:

The Science of Super-Geography

And all these things falling out of the sky, he says, is what causes star-jelly, star-rot, star-slubber, whatever you call it: it is the stuff brought down in meteor falls. Or so says Fort. Quite wrongly, obviously.

Obviously, says Myra. What jelly?

He finds a photo on his phone – it's like it looks, gloopy, translucent stuff, sicked up by herons, I think. It doesn't appear very often, but there was a lot of it about this year earlier on. I've got some people in the Natural History section of the museum working on it. Or possibly not. I think they've probably lost it. That's why I was going in, he added, when I saw you that time.

I don't remember.

No. You were very upset. You didn't see me.

There is a powerful silence from the bed. He looks at her sideways. You can't get any paler, woman, he thinks. Stop it. Now.

Something happened in there, didn't it? What idiocy made him ask her that? He is braced for something sharp, something bitter, in response. But she just sounds genuinely puzzled.

In where?

In the museum. You were coming down the steps.

Oh… I see. No. No. I don't go in.

What, never? He is astonished again.

No. Why? Should I?

I… well, No. I just thought you spent a lot of time there.

I do. But not inside. And anyway, she adds suspiciously, how do you know I am there a lot?

Theo shrugs, busy puzzling something out. A man called Luke. American. iPad.

Is he a friend of yours?

No. Not at all, I met him once.

And you talked about *me*? Are you here because of him? Her eyes are dark smudges, she is weak and wild, and they are both trembling on the verge of not understanding each other at all. He gets suddenly to his feet, a baffled giant, and walks angrily two or three times around the foot of her bed. Then he stops and looks down at her, directly into her face.

I am here, he says, because my mother is ill. The rest is coincidence. Believe that, or don't believe it, as you wish; it isn't important. What is important is that something happened to you in the…

And it dawns on him.

…*no*, on the steps of the museum, just outside, wasn't it? Myra. Myra listen. I think I know what happened. Tell me. It was just outside, wasn't it?

She will not look at him looking at her, stares fiercely at the empty wall ahead.

He will miss his train, he thinks. He doesn't know if he can leave her. He is not angry now. *Oh Myra, what is the matter with you?* He reaches for his bag and the book, and puts his jacket on.

I have to go, he says, more gently. But I'll come back tomorrow, and I think, if you won't tell me, that I can tell you what happened on the steps. But this is too much now. I'll come back. Get some sleep.

When she finally looks up at him her eyes are wet with tears.

It doesn't want me, she says.

25.

They set out again through the busy streets. He guides her a complicated route, picking out a path against the traffic and the people through the maze of silent threads. Sometimes he warns her when they are about to cross one, or briefly follow a trail; sometimes he doesn't tell her, and watches to see how she reacts. Some seem to slip past her without making a mark, but others cause a ripple of concentration across her face. She turns to him for confirmation; he nods and shows her the map. They visit several of Luke's benches, each caught in a noose of silence, their sitters vanished or moved on. She has put her phone away in her coat pocket and started using her hands to drop occasional comments into the air. A few of her phrases come back to him, half-remembered, he has forgotten the language, but her expressive face tells him most of what he needs to know. His own hands hover close in the air around her, and he guides her through town with the gentlest touch of her elbow, a brush of fingers on her coat.

Outside the museum, though, he stops and begins to text again. He tells her about the thick wall of silence wrapped like a huge snake around the building; his team, he says, have been monitoring it. He finds a recent report in his emails and hands her the phone for her to read it: it is putting the public off, they think, even though most of them don't notice it; it seems to be turning them away at some subconscious level, you can see them on the steps hovering about and changing their minds. The museum authorities are very concerned about the effect on footfall, especially with the Easter holidays coming up. Staff, says the report, are demoralised; a lot are phoning in sick.

She nods and hands back the phone. Stands with her hands deep in the pockets of her big coat and looks at the building critically for a few moments, before making her way very slowly up the steps. He stands on the red tarmac, watching her.

She halts two or three steps from the top and puts a hand on the railing, as if to steady herself, stays very still for a few seconds and then turns and heads back down to the road with a cold, sour look on her face. She shakes her head as if to throw off an unpleasantness, and her eyes tell him she doesn't know what is going on. He smiles and takes one of her cold hands between both of his and lifts it briefly to his lips. None of us know, he says. It's unsettling us all.

Strong enough for the castle? It's nearly half past.

She nods.

They ignore the sideways underpass and head decisively straight ahead. And then stand, foolishly, as people always do, balanced on the knobbly kerb of the A470 waiting for the sudden inrush of traffic in both directions to abate. She texts him as they stand.

How did you get the castle to open?!

Sold my soul.

You haven't got one.

They don't know that.

No really how?

Really. Have to do weekend shooting pheasants in Scotland.

Christ in heaven… Shoot to miss!

Will do… The pheasants, anyway.

When they look up again they see they have missed the lull: cars and buses roar past in opposing streams, impossible. He grabs her arm and points back to the underpass, and they set off, half-running, laughing, their hands colliding softly, then pulling away.

A man in a dark-blue uniform is waiting for them outside the castle. They apologise for being a little late, and show their identity cards. That's all right, sir, says the man, looking at them both. But I'm afraid I do have to lock up at six.

That's fine, says the professor, I don't think we'll need long.

The uniformed man pulls an electronic key-card from his breast pocket, and the small wooden door cut into the huge oak door of the entrance swings open.

There you are, sir, he says. All yours. The grounds, that is: you know the buildings are locked up?

Yes, they told me. We just need a quick look at the grounds this time. Thank you.

I'll be waiting out here, says the man. I'll call at five to, if you're not done by then.

Fine, says the professor, and steps through the doorway with Meg.

It is the first time he has been inside since the Norman keep was removed piece by carefully labelled piece and despatched to America, over a decade ago, to pay for a new wing on the hospital; he is shocked by the flattened, grassed-over space and the damp ditch of the moat, sitting in the huge empty green square inside the walls. They feel the sudden drop in temperature and look at each other. He raises his eyebrows and gestures that they should walk round the outer gravel path, past dilapidated buildings where he remembers a café and a gift shop: wooden swords, plastic helmets. She slips her hand into his and they walk together, quiet and concentrating, and climb the grassy bank to the walls and walk along the top looking down. It feels easier to breathe up there.

They come down again to the level, where Meg gently pulls him to a halt.

Just me now, she says with her hands. He nods and lets her go, but he is tight with anxiety. The place is awash with silence, so thick he can feel it in his lungs. He keeps his eyes fixed on her, the strongest, the fiercest person he knows, walking across the grass towards the centre of the green space, towards the emptied moat which had once protected the vanished keep. Where he and his brother had climbed like wicked goats. His frightened mother.

She slows down by the wooden bridge that crosses the moat. And begins to talk with her hands. Not to him, he's pretty sure of that. Phrases flash out at him like glimpses of light, like birds too quick for him to identify; this is complex, agitated language. He can't see her face, but can sense her distress. He is half-aware of time passing too quickly; they must only have a few minutes left. He watches from the foot of the bank with growing concern, urgently waiting for a sign that he can move again.

At last she turns. She has raised her hands to her ears as if to shut out a terrible noise. Like that bloody Munch painting, he thinks, as he sets off quickly across the grass towards her. And then she sways, and he breaks into a run, and catches her, and pulls her into him and holds her very tight. *Dere*, he says, *dere nawr*. They make for the open door. It seems miles. And the word in his head, over and over, is his mother's: *annifyr*.

26.

Dan has just sat down on Myra's bench, as an experiment. Teddy is making his way round the circular flowerbed with the standing stones, stopping to examine things, talking to himself.

No! says Dan. *Dim yn dy geg!* Don't put it in your mouth... And for once, he doesn't.

Then suddenly there is Theo looming over him, looking

faintly shocked.

Hello, says Dan – are you on your way in or out?

Neither, says Theo. I came to sit here a moment. He doesn't say why, doesn't say that her bed is empty and that she has disappeared.

Then sit. You'll find it's cold.

After a minute or so they look at each other and get up. Dan suggests following Teddy round the flowerbed, so they pace round the stones, past dark budding tulips and brash primulas, and talk. Dan tells him about the emptying benches, the people vanishing. At least we know where *she is*, he says, gesturing to the bench. Have you seen her?

Theo nods, noncommittally.

Is she OK?

I don't know.

Do you think they'll all end up in hospital, then?

Doesn't seem terribly likely does it? No. I expect the cold feeling just moves them on.

Dan tells him that Luke says they have a plan, at the department, that the professor has an idea for some Arts Intervention scheme, dancing or something, to try and tackle it.

Theo looks sceptical. They tried all that stuff years ago, in the depression, you remember? Or perhaps you're too young. People dancing and reading all over the place, you couldn't move for performances.

Teddy has to be restrained from biting the head off a tulip.

Not too young. Think I probably performed with the best of them; I expect I was excruciating. But I don't think we did any harm.

Hmm. Well it didn't exactly work, did it?

Maybe not, maybe a bit.

62

They watch a dog and its owner manoeuvre nervously past the child.

What do you do for a living? asks Dan.

Theo explains about the organisation, the official part of it at least, and tells him about the nature reserve and the pool and the wetlands. We do a lot of conservation stuff with schools, he says. Kids can come out, help plant trees, catalogue wildlife. We get some public money to do that, and then there are private projects, ponds, mini-reserves, landscaping. And we salve bad consciences: companies, individuals. Planting trees is like saying hail-marys, only more productive.

Are you a big team, then? asks Dan.

Never enough of us, says Theo. And since my mother broke her hip I've let far too much go. I can't concentrate. It's pretty hard staying on top of everything at the moment.

It must be.

He doesn't say it, but he thinks in a vague unformed way that he would be glad to feel like that, to have too much to do, the urgency of it. Not that he hasn't got too much to do with the house and Teddy, but to have other people waiting for you, needing you to do things for them, that must not be a bad thing. A public sphere. When all the benches are empty, he thinks, I'll be no use to anyone except Teddy, who is a different kind of sphere, the whole round world, the whole wide universe, the Alpha and Omega. Little bugger that he is.

He removes another piece of tulip from the child's mouth. Finds a dinosaur in his pocket and offers him that instead.

How about you? says Theo, sensing something in Dan's pause.

Work? No. Not at the moment. It's all him.

You're on your own, aren't you? Theo tries to remember the conversation on the steps.

Yes. Yes, it's nearly two years since his mother died.

Ah. That's difficult.

But before that I was in literature, a researcher. And she was an astrophysicist.

Oh yes, I remember, I saw you in there by the meteors.

They walked round again.

But I'll need to do something soon, says Dan. We're barely managing, and they'll stop all the benefits when he turns two unless I register for work.

Teddy falls over and howls. Dan picks him up and fetches wipes from the buggy, cleans the grazed hand. He sets him down again with a kiss. You stink, he says. We'll have to go back in there and change you.

What will you do? asks Theo. Will you try the University again?

No, I've been too long out of the system, and I didn't finish my project because Jane got ill. They don't fund failures. And anyway I couldn't do it any more; it's ended. Not me.

So what would you like to do?

He sounds genuinely interested, thinks Dan, with a small rush of gratitude. He smiles and shrugs, and holds his hands up in front of him.

Use these, he says. The head is fucked. The rest of me is tired, but recoverable, probably.

Come and spend a day with us, then, says Theo. See what you think. We need hands.

27.

Hunkered down at the edge of the pond he lets the water run through his fingers and examines the wriggling larvae in the clay and silt left in the palm of his big hand. Life enough there. He transfers the clay to the small tank beside him, and scoops up another handful; same again but different. A little fish is trapped in the mud this time, and he washes it free. He looks up with a grin as a scud of starlings fling themselves like some kind of self-conscious magic trick across the pond and off into the far line of trees. They break his concentration, so he gets up and stretches his aching knee, and wonders what next. He should go inside and make something to eat, he is getting cold, and his jeans are wet from kneeling. But he is still too restless to go in; he needs to walk, he decides, up the hill, a proper fierce walk that will erase the nightmarish quality of the day's walking in the white corridors.

He had gone back the following day, unable to sleep for concern; her pinched unhappy face, those tears. He'd gone back to tell her about the network of silence, to try and understand her distress a little more. The curtains had been drawn around the bed when he arrived, and he had spent a patient hour reading to his mother, and answering questions, as best he could, on behalf of his dead but increasingly present younger brother. And when he had finished, and gone back to Myra's part of the ward, the curtains had still been drawn. On the train home he had cancelled the following morning's meetings and laboriously reorganised a pond-drop all for nothing. The bed, the following day, was clean and empty. No sign of her things. No sign of her.

He asked the nurses on the ward, none of whom he

recognised. No one seemed to know what had happened to Myra, and more urgent things were happening to other people, and even the sympathetic ones could not stay to help. Back down at reception, after a painful wait, he had spoken to someone behind a desk with a huge computer screen. Myra Jones. Admitted about a fortnight, three weeks, ago. Has she been discharged? They were experiencing technical problems, said the woman. Serious problems, affecting their data. From what she could see they had no record of anybody with that name, but she couldn't give a definitive answer, given the chaos. Come back later.

So he had walked white corridors, all of them too much alike, level upon level, and scanned all the wards he could get into with a cold fear growing inside him. He had left the building defeated and angry, but certain that she was still in it. Which hadn't stopped him helplessly making the detour to her bench, just in case.

He is starving. The need for food is making him shake. He has worked hard, thinking, to keep her white face at bay, of Dan in the park, wondering what on earth they will do with Teddy, if he comes. He wants tea and toast, and his mother's marmalade; probably the last she will ever make now, the kitchen full of its citrus smell and the glorious array of jars just days before her fall. It should be hoarded like dragon gold; but today he needs its warmth. He should go in and light the fire now; the sun is going down behind the hill.

But he sets off instead for the far line of trees on the ridge, where the starlings were headed, walking hard and fast. Past the brave damson with its white stars. His hand in his jacket pocket finds a metal ring, the silver twisted bracelet. There was no story attached, it transpired. She had looked at it quite blankly, and reached out for the river pearls instead, running them with pleasure from hand to hand and talking in the mildly scolding tone of voice she kept for his father; he had a job on his hands, these days, representing so many ghosts. So he could do what he liked with it, he thinks, reaching the foot of the hill, and the grove of slightly older trees, the three, four, five year olds: stronger, taller, harder to transplant, but that much more of a triumph when it works. And more expensive for the sinners, of course; more hail-marys for your money.

And as the light of day gradually drains out of the darkening grove and into the far pond, he finds what he has been looking for, a particular silver-grey rowan, its pale clusters not ready yet to flower, but looking promising enough. He pulls a springy branch down towards him and carefully slips the bracelet on. Pushes it down, gently negotiating the little lateral buds and twigs, until it settles nicely, a silver twist against the smooth grey-brown bark. He admires it in the vanishing light. Grins at another sudden volley of starlings, and turns back towards the house.

28.

The face she sees is not the face she wanted to see, so she closes her eyes briefly and tries again. She is, in any case, still trying to untangle herself from a word she has heard somewhere and does not understand, *genesistrine*, sticky as a cobweb in her mind. But when she opens her eyes a second time, and focuses, it is still the wrong one, though familiar enough: a dark-brown bob cut so beautifully it slides like silk against the strong face with the pale blue eyes that bends over her all sympathy and concern.

Hello Myra, says the senior colleague. How are you feeling now? You have had a rough time.

Myra smiles weakly and nods and shrugs and looks self-deprecating all at once.

We thought we'd lost you! said the colleague. Not like that, I mean, though the consultant just told me they were worried you were too weak for this operation; he's a nice man, isn't he? We had a good chat. No, literally lost you – you got blipped off the system in some data-crash, did you know? No one could remember which ward you were supposed to be on, and Elin went all over gynaecology yesterday looking, and said you definitely weren't where she'd left you last week, and then I thought I bet it's cancer, and struck lucky up here. I always did think you might be the type. You poor girl.

She settles down in the chair by Myra's bed. It looks like the same chair, thinks Myra, slowly, same chair same table same bed, but the light's all wrong, the window is in a different place. Much closer. She can see out over a flat roof to brick buildings and a skyline of sorts, quite a bit of pale sky. Rain on the glass.

It's raining, she says, quietly.

I won't stay long this time, says the senior colleague, I have to get Siân from gymnastics. She's got an exam next week, it's going incredibly well, when you think she just started this year; I'm so proud of her, don't know where she gets it from. But here, I've brought you this, from all of us.

She pulls out some flowers and a card. Myra opens the envelope and is surprisingly moved to see how many people have signed it. Although, on reflection, she suspects they probably didn't have much choice.

And this from me of course! Producing a cake wrapped in foil and zipped into a plastic freezer bag. For when you feel a bit stronger, it keeps quite well. Apple, my mother's recipe, Robbie and Siân's favourite. I had to make two this time, or they wouldn't have let me leave the house, you know what kids are like.

Thank you, says Myra. Lovely.

Yes. You do need building up ... I always thought you were thin before but look at you now. Does it hurt, you know, where they operated?

Not sure, says Myra. I'm on painkillers, I think.

I expect you are, says the colleague. Terrible.

And then, reaching out to pat her arm, the concern spreading thickly all over her face again, We are so sorry. And you're so young! It happened to a friend of mine but she was in her fifties and had three kids; it's so terrible to think you can never have children...

I haven't really thought about it, says Myra.

You can always adopt, she says; another friend did, it's very rewarding. And anyway, maybe you're not the maternal type, you know. Not everyone is.

She gets up and collects her things, then turns back brightly: And just think, you won't ever need to worry about contraception!

Myra doesn't know what to say.

When she has gone Myra goes back to the business of

getting her bearings. She has, she realises, been here perhaps a couple of days already, but too ill and drugged to care. This ward is higher up, she reckons. And having the window that much closer is interesting. A huge gull is stamping up and down on the flat roof just outside. The sky is still completely devoid of colour. It looks cold.

When a nurse comes with fresh water for the bedside jug and a vase for the flowers she asks her to take the cake away and share it with the other nurses. That makes her feel better, for a while. She thinks with a kind of distant amusement how the news of her ovaries will be transmitted around the office, and then, thinking of the office, she sees her desk and her computer, and cannot help but imagine the rising tide of emails building up inside the machine, pushing and pushing to be released. When she goes back to work and switches the computer on, she thinks, they will surge out in a huge black wave and smash her against the wall, breaking her fragile bones.

She cringes back into the pillows and prays for sleep to come. Which, miraculously, it does.

29.

She is on her silent train heading for a silent Paris, he thinks; perhaps at this moment she is under the sea rushing towards the city with its grand and heartless perspectives, its distinctive smells. He wants to text her so she knows he is with her every mile, every kilometre of the way; that he watches her watching the world crammed into the jolting metro, and that he can climb every bit as lightly as she can up every single step out into the cold air and the blur and rush of evening lights. He wants to tell her to have a glass of beer for him in the place on the corner. He wants to know if she will be able to see the Chagall exhibition between rehearsals.

But not one of those silver threads gets sent, because he is working, and she is too, and he must turn his whole attention to the questions of his unsettled staff and the demands of unsettled ministers, and prepare for separate hurried meetings with the representatives of the museum board, and university high command, and the bloke from the council, and the army, and the journalists, and the television people, and all the others. He ticks off in his head the people who will need persuading in the next few hours, wonders how best to group them to get the best results and save time. But he does re-read the three notes she sent from St Pancras – the first an electronic scribble looped like a ribbon round a capital M, and underneath it the words: *Fill it with noise*. And then the second, qualifying: *The loop, I mean: not the M*. And finally, the single word: *Parade*.

How about we get the schoolchildren to hold hands round the building and sing? Phoebe is as button-bright as ever.

I thought the idea was to keep everyone moving? says someone else. We don't want them to get trampled.

Yes, it's a parade, remember; everyone needs to keep marching, singing, yelling, whatever…

Should they all be singing from the same hymn sheet? asks Aslan. Metaphorically, I mean.

Why metaphorically? It wouldn't be a bad idea – *ddim yn ffôl o gwbl t'wbod. Beth am Calon Lân?*

Not multicultural enough? Luke sounds faintly apologetic.

Ond mae pawb yn hoffi Calon Lân! We could have the Merthyr Male Voice…

Colliery bands!

No, no, says Aslan: I think we need to be *more angry*: more in your face, I mean in its face, you know what I mean. Like punk, or Pussy Riot, or the early days of Brith Gof. We should bang things. Car doors. Oil drums.

That sounds satisfyingly medieval. *Charivari.*

Mari Lwyd!

The lot, throw the lot at it. Dylan as well, full blast. A hundred drama students all reciting *Under Milk Wood*. Or wait, 'Do Not Go Gentle', even better. That should finish it off. The Death of Silence.

The professor flexes a hand and gets to his feet and writes a beautiful black M on the whiteboard; then draws a fluent loop around it, with an arrow to show the direction of travel, clockwise. Underneath, he writes the words: Fill it with noise. Above, in a firm hand, he writes *Cacoffoni Cymru: Wales Wails*. There is a wholly spontaneous cheer.

30.

Luke is in the Kitty O'Shea, with his second pint of something that is still, after seven years, slightly too authentic for him. He will get there. He loves this place, this country, too much not to acquire its tastes. He is working, sort of, on a précis of the Parade meeting, and dipping in and out of the most recent maps of the silence, and sending a few emails to get ahead of himself for more meetings tomorrow. But he wishes he had someone real to sit next to. The noise levels surge and fall around him, like waves on shingle. It isn't a young crowd, in here. And mostly men. Some in suits, maybe with a journalist amongst them. Some scruffier ones, laughing at each other, trading insults. One curious pair, a man and a woman, talking with a kind of starry intensity; others sitting together in the kind of social British silence he has yet to figure out. It feels warm in here, it feels good; there is some undefinable Irish-sounding music washing out from the back. He looks at the portraits of Kitty and Parnell, facing each other bravely from opposite walls. He raises his glass to them both, he wishes them luck.

After a while he comes to realise that the person he would most like to share this drink with is Dan. Which is a non-starter, of course, it being dark and cold and past nine, and the Kitty O' Shea not being a suitable venue for a toddler. He starts to text a cheerful, slightly laboured message, about meeting up soon, and how he has news to report, and how he hopes they're doing fine … and then, suddenly, he stops texting and presses call.

The place is much too noisy for this, he thinks, too late, and presses one hand over his other ear, and leans forward looking pained. He can hardly hear whether it is ringing or not at the other end, and wonders, in a rush of regret at his own impulsiveness, if he'll be able to hear anything even if Dan does pick up. Which he doesn't.

Luke puts the phone down on the table rather sadly, and has another sip of beer, and wonders if it might in fact be off, and wonders how you'd ever know. And he is just thinking about the best way to finish and send the original cheery text when the phone starts ringing.

Dan sounds utterly panicked.

What's happened? He says. What is it?

Luke clamps his hand over his free ear.

Nothing's happened. I just wanted to … ah … say hello.

Fuck's sake, Luke! Nobody *ever* rings this thing. I thought someone had died.

No, no, says Luke. I … ah … just thought we should catch up. I'm sorry, I didn't mean…

It's OK, says Dan. No. It's OK. It's fine.

I'll … ah … text tomorrow then? If you're busy now, I mean…

Busy! says Dan, sounding slightly bitter. No. No, he's down now. I'm not busy. As such.

Ah. I'm in a pub, says Luke. I just thought it would make a change from coffee, but I know it's not … ah…

There is nothing, says Dan, very emphatically, there is nothing I would like more at this moment than a pint in a noisy pub. But not possible. Ring again in about ten years' time.

I'm sorry, says Luke.

Where are you then? Which one?

Luke tells him.

That's ten minutes from me, man, says Dan. Fifteen at the most. You come here instead. Less noisy, unless he wakes up. Bring beer, or Coke, or whatever it is Californians drink. I'll text you the address and you can google your way over in the dark.

I'm drinking beer, says Luke, proudly. But I'll bring both.

31.

She is stuck, once again, at the clinging edges of a bad dream. A weed-ridden sea, that won't let her through in either direction; not forwards, to the land which she would like to reach and which she knows is close; not back into the dream, whose keynote is a sadness as wide and as bleak as the open ocean. And so everything is neither one thing nor the other, unless it is both. The figure of the man leaning intently over the naked woman is both sculptor and surgeon, about to do what he has to do to save her. He has a white marble beard, all coiled and curled, or a surgical face-mask, and he reaches out now to touch her, to roll her gently back towards him, so he can finish the job.

The woman is lovely. Marble again, lying on her side with her head resting on one arm, facing away. Her right hip disappears into, or has not yet been released from, the rough block of white stone. Sculpted strands of hair fall round her neck, her shoulders, and frame the face that looks away with an expression of unutterable distance and sadness. Seen from this angle, the curved body is not what it seemed; it is not relaxed, nor sleepily coming alive: it is tense and expectant. Her lips are pressed thin and her eyes stare straight ahead.

It is not his fault, she understands that much, thrashing

about with some irritation in the weed. He is the creator, after all, yes even when he is more surgeon than sculptor, bent over the white anaesthetised body with a fine-bladed knife, she knows he is giving her the chance to carry on living and breathing, and what statue, however obstinate, would not jump at the chance to pull free of the marble block? Her ingratitude is devastating, he must never see it; so she keeps her face turned away and hopes her curves will be enough of a disguise, and that when the gentle hand eventually touches the marble flank she will not, this time, freeze and cry out.

Not again, he thinks, and wonders if he should get a nurse. She is clearly distressed and dreaming, her body curled protectively under the covers, her restless face expecting the worst. But she is not shouting, not yet; he watches a moment to see if it will pass. His big hands grip the metal bed-frame. He should call her, he thinks.

This time, though, she pulls herself free, and begins to wake into the bright sunlight of the ward. He stands quietly at the foot of her bed and waits to be recognised, watching as her thin mouth relaxes and the laughter, like water, rises slowly in her green eyes.

32.

Dan is so astonished to see the Syrian woman again he holds out his arms and almost embraces her; she looks up at him surprised, and he puts a hand on her shoulder and presses it gently. When she sees who it is she smiles a big smile, and raises her hands, and says she has no sweets for them this time. She looks older.

Oh, says Dan, parking Teddy neatly by the bench, I'm so glad you're here. We missed you. Your bench has been empty for days – all the benches – I mean, I thought you were gone.

Not yet, she says. Maybe never. She reaches over to stroke Teddy's hair.

Well, I'm glad anyway. How are you?

She shrugs. It's OK, she says. OK. You know?

I know. He sits down next to her and shivers. Have you heard from your son? She shakes her head. And the others – the ones in Palestine?

No. Not recently.

The cold air around the bench defies the late April sun. Lina al Hassan has tears in her eyes.

I wanted almond blossom, she says; now I want apricot blossom. I have a grand-daughter I have never seen.

Dan bows his head, then gets up and extricates the un-usually placid Teddy from the buggy. Praying that he will co-operate, he gives him a biscuit and puts him carefully into her lap. He doesn't try to wriggle free, and by the time he has eaten his biscuit has discovered the bright stones in the rings on her worn-out hands. Lapis lazuli, opal, amethyst.

Thank you.

He can tell from her voice, from the soft curve of her arm, how the comfortable weight of the boy in her lap fills a void. It is her turn to ask:

How are you?

And his turn to shrug. OK, he says. It's OK. All my time is with him, I don't do much else. Are you working at the moment?

She nods. Still cleaning at the hospital, a few hours a week. It's fine; the girls are fun. I don't mind it at all.

Did you work before? Back home, I mean.

She nods, looks almost abashed.

University lecturer.

Christ, says Dan. What in?

Microbiology.

They look at each other and see the absurdity of it and start laughing.

Come on, says Dan. Let me buy you a coffee in the park.

She raises her thick black eyebrows and looks almost fierce. Because I'm a university lecturer?

No, he says, because this bench is bloody cold and just through that big gate there I promise it is actually spring.

I don't have a swipe-card, she says. I'm not, how do you say, legitimate.

Don't worry, says Dan. I know other ways.

33.

You took some finding, he says.

I heard I had disappeared.

They look at each other, delighted. He bends over to kiss her lightly on the cheek and is ambushed by thin arms which suddenly hug him tight.

Thank you for finding me, she says, I was afraid you might never come.

No chance of that, he says. No chance at all. I've got too much to tell you; it's been building in my head. Like water behind a dam.

So tell me, she says, pulling herself more upright and patting the arm of the chair. No, wait. Go and get a cup of tea, and let me do my hair.

He grins and gives an ironic half-bow, and heads off in search of tea. Myra hauls herself further up and carefully puts her legs over the side of the bed, and sits for a few seconds, waiting to see what will happen next. Nothing. Good. She bends extremely cautiously to pull open the door of the locker by the bed where her things are, and is feeling around awkwardly inside when the distant buzzing starts up, and she gets a dim sense of the encroaching shadow. She curses, knowing she should retreat and get her legs back on the bed and lie flat as quickly as she can, but she thinks she can feel the spines of the brush, and tries to race the pooling dark as you might race an incoming tide in a place, like a channel or a sandbar, where the water comes from many directions.

So when he comes back with a small tray and two mugs and some standard-issue biscuits she is not in the bed, but beside it, with her arms wrapped around her knees and her head down and her whole body shaking.

Myra, for god's sake!

He puts the tray down and crouches beside her, and when she lifts her face to his she is tear-stained and laughing.

What happened?

She waves the hairbrush at him.

Got the bastard, she says.

She won't let him ring for the nurse, but she does let him help her back into bed and give her a mug of horrible sweet tea and a brief homily on the virtues of patience in patients.

There's no time to be patient, I have no time for this. She is helpless, petulant.

Tough, he says. If you're not patient now there'll be no time for anything later.

She shrugs, and then sips her tea. Decides not to tell him that one of the consultants is advising a course of chemotherapy.

Tell me the other things now, she says, the ones behind the dam. And he starts to explain about the channels of silence eating into the city, and tells her a bit about Luke and Dan, and the other people on the benches, and the mapping project, and the various possible solutions, including the imminent parade around the museum. He treads as carefully as he can, nervous of upsetting her, but she nods, and seems to accept it all without difficulty, and even laughs at the idea of the parade.

That poor building, she says. Doesn't sound at all like its kind of thing. Undignified. Do you think it'll work?

Theo considers. No, he says. No, I don't. I'm not sure that even they think it will really. The problem is obviously next door, and the solution obviously needs to be more radical. But I think it's a useful experiment, to see if noise is the answer, if it helps at all. And it'll be vastly entertaining to watch.

Are you going?

I thought I probably would. It'll be on telly, though – you can watch it from here. Saturday. Day after tomorrow.

I'm unlikely to be out by then.

On your current showing, most unlikely.

She closes her eyes. I'm going to sleep again, she says. Then, anxiously. Will you still be here when I wake up?

He looks at his phone. Probably not, he says. I have heaps to do. But I'll stay till you're properly asleep, and I promise you the dream won't…

It was a different one, she says, visibly drifting now. It was sad, sad… She looks at him from a distance and he can see trouble fogging up her eyes.

Not now, he says. Don't try and tell me now. I'll come back tomorrow and maybe you can tell me then; here, let me read a bit, close your eyes, here's some more Fort.

34.

They finally work their way through the last item on the list and rub their eyes and look at each other. Finished. Yes. Thank you.

They stand up, and he puts a friendly hand on Luke's shoulder and thanks him again, warmly, for all his hard work. The look he receives is so proud, so helplessly grateful, it pulls him up short. He smiles him out of the office and turns back to his desk, glad, half-amused, a little shocked, to have made the young man so happy: that such things should be somehow in his gift still surprises him. It has been a pleasure, too; he is so used to having negotiate resistance.

He stands perfectly still at his desk for a moment, letting it all ebb away. The week-long frenzy of meetings, of organization, is still flinging out a few last-minute emails; they drop quietly onto his computer screens, his phone, his iPad. He deliberately disconnects. He turns off his computer, watches the beautiful maps go out one after the other all around the room, puts his work phone into a drawer, and then, next to it, his private phone. He leaves the drawer open for a minute or two, while he slowly unknots his tie, just in case her name should light up either of them. You could wish me luck, he thinks. It was your idea. He pushes the drawer to, slips out of his neat dark jacket, hangs it carefully on the back of his chair. Then he unbuttons his white shirt and takes that off too. He sits at his desk, putting one foot, then the other, onto his desk to remove his shoes and his bright socks. Then he stands, his bare feet on the smooth cold floor, to unbuckle his belt and slip out of his trousers, folding them neatly over the chair. He spends five minutes prowling around the room in his boxers and t-shirt, opens the drawer one last time, and shuts it hard. You could wish me luck. He fetches his running things from the cupboard and puts them on; finds his swipe-card and his housekey, pushes them deep into the pocket of his shorts, and heads out towards the park.

There is little point in running before the park itself. He crosses the war memorial gardens as briskly as he can; another place where the cold silence pools, and the thick white cherry blossom seems unreal, suspended. He nods at the high naked angel with the beautiful wings and the beautiful behind. *Ti ddim yn oer lan fan 'na ngwas i?* The A470 opens up for him like the Red Sea, and he is suddenly at the gates.

There, with his usual ironic grimace, he swipes his card and he is in, running fast and light across the playing fields through bright trees and rugby players, children, sweet hyacinths and dogs, to the river. The great park swindle, he thinks, still not quite yet apparent. Give it another couple of years. It depends how quickly people, the People, decide to sell up. He has been pushing at the university council for months now to do what he has done in the Institute, and start buying them whenever and wherever they come up – in twos and threes, if necessary, though occasionally you'll get a small handful, all at once. People die, or suddenly need the money; they can always borrow a card from a friend, from a relation; or they never go near the place at all, why would they? Cash it in now. It's just a matter of time, of patience.

The river calms him; he forgets his anger and the daft complexities of tomorrow's parade in the noise of the breath in his lungs and the feel of the late afternoon sun on his back and arms. He drifts over to Paris, stands on a dusky corner in an interesting hat and watches her coming up the street laughing silently with her friends; her glance raised to meet his shocks them both; her agility on the stage, twenty years ago. Birds sing in the trees all around him. He runs for many miles, following the river, looping, diverting, making it last: he comes out at length into a network of terraces and back lanes, and weaves his way home.

He showers, cooks, and lies down on the sofa to watch the news; perhaps he sleeps for an hour. At around midnight he leaves the house again to cycle across the quiet city.

Back in the silent building he spends a couple of hours dealing with the final emails; there are no real crises, no major names bailing out, no helicopters pulled from the sky for technical reasons. He sends calm and concise answers to those who will need them in the morning. Then he sets his many maps to brighten the room in their different colours, fading in and out, chasing, overlaid, gradually replaced: he sees, over and over, how the channels of silence are like the branching capillaries of lungs. At around two he packs it all up again, closes it down, locks up and leaves. And as he heads down the stairs the phone in his breast pocket pulses. He smiles and pulls it out, still lit up from the inside. *Pob lwc*, she says.

35.

The buggy and the sleeping child are parked tidily in a corner of the town library. Dan sits at a crowdsource workstation, dragging white ellipses over star-clusters with a practised hand and eye. He is somewhere in the Horseshoe Nebula, identifying anomalies for the Mapping the Heavens project, refreshing his memory with the names of certain stars, the nature and shapes of the swirling phenomena of deep space, so that he will be able to teach them to Teddy when he is older. They don't teach this stuff at school, do they; he wonders why ever not. Since he stopped paying for an internet connection at home, and since his laptop packed up, these workstations, scattered all over the city, are a lifeline, a proper lifeline, not a manner of speaking; just as the child himself is a lifeline. And so is music, and beer. He used to spend his evenings doing this, but now it's down to two or three sessions in the early afternoon, after Mother and Toddler group, when Teddy is properly worn out and his nap is deep and lasts a good hour. Long enough to get lost in space. Parent and Toddler, he means; Parent-stroke-Guardian and Toddler. There are quite a few grand-parents too, of course, the parents are all out working, poor sods. As he should be, as he will be, soon.

Today it is harder to concentrate. He breaks every ten minutes to check for messages, and finds only disappoint-ment. His sister in London is busy for the forseeable future. His parents-in-law have failed, as ever, to take the hint. Un-fair. They are both ill, and old, and could not manage him for a whole day in any case, not now that he is running around. And they don't change nappies. And, to be per-fectly honest, Teddy barely knows them. There are the play-group mothers, of course. The concerned, flirtatious mothers. One of them would take him for a morning or af-ternoon, he thinks. But, given the travelling, he needs a whole day. A whole day would be too much. And in the quick rush of frustration and anger that follows he realises, with a helpless falling-away like sand slipping under your feet as you climb a dune, that he is not yet ready to leave the child with anyone else, not for a morning, not for an af-ternoon, not yet.

Tears force their way into his eyes. He gets up and walks over to get a drink of water. And as if he really can see from the back of his head, he catches the sense of a big shape lumbering over towards Teddy's pushchair. He turns very quickly and is about to cut back across the room when recognition holds him back: it is the black guy from the bench near the church, smiling and crooning and holding one of his cut-out pictures. He lays it very gently on the boy's stomach, and winks and bows at Dan, then ambles out, collecting his fat plastic bags from under a table near the door. Dan goes over to the child, still deeply asleep, and picks up the ragged cut-out, which is of a bird, a blackbird in a tree. It has a bright-eyed, university prospectus look about it. Teddy will be delighted.

Blessed by the encounter, Dan goes back to his stars with renewed commitment. And as he sizes and sorts them, he thinks of the constant mild shock, the oddness, of seeing any of the bench people out of their highly restricted context. It happens surprisingly infrequently. And then he thinks of the last time he saw the black guy, on his bench, singing and talking to himself and all the passing shoppers. It was sunny. People were responding cheerily. He had stood up unexpectedly, begun ceremoniously removing coats, three of them, each one filthy, and each one an entirely different sort of coat: a thick parka anorak; an oversized suit jacket, a big winter coat, in no logical order. He just adds layers, thinks Dan, as the benches get colder. The silence won't be driving him away just yet. But some of the others, he feels, won't be coming back. He thinks the red-haired boy is probably dead. And the busker is restless, constantly shifting his patch, his songs sounding less and less convincing.

Where we are   is among the stars

Then, somewhere deep in the Trifid Nebula, Dan thinks of Lina, and sees in a burst of clarity that she could be the answer to his problem.

36.

Long dull-red hairs choke up the bristles of the brush. She picks at them with a shudder of hopelessness, and puts another clump of hair in the bin beside her bed. A tangle of red against the layer of crumpled tissues. And under the white of the tissues, more tangled red, then more crumpled white. And so on. Stop brushing your hair, she thinks. And stop crying.

She has a thirst on her that cannot be cured by water. She cannot stop thinking about fresh lemons. Squeezed over ice-cubes. The smell of grated zest. Boiled in their skins with a bit of sugar for old-fashioned lemonade. She thinks of lemon trees, the scent of their dark glossy leaves crushed. And she thinks, so much does she crave the taste, that she could probably suck half a lemon now, without her mouth twisting in shock.

Today she submits to the morning's rituals without a word. Painkillers, blood-pressure, temperature. The nurse worries vaguely that this obedience might be a bad sign, but does not fuss her with questions. Everyone is excited about the parade, and at ten those who are well enough to move pile into the dayroom to watch the half-hour of build-up before the event begins. Those still in their beds are set up with extra pillows and the screen on the wall is adjusted to suit. In Myra's room the nurse turns the sound off and places the remote control beside her; there are still fifteen minutes to go. Then she goes off to fetch her a cup of tea, and Myra hasn't the heart to tell her, when it arrives, that she wants lemon in it, not milk.

All is quiet for five minutes, and then the cleaner arrives, apologetic. They are all quite out of their routine, this morning, she says; they have had to do some sections as a priority, before the parade, and they are short-staffed because several people wanted the morning off to see it. It's fine, Myra says, I'm not really sure I'm watching it. Please go ahead. The woman nods and smiles. Empties the bin of its red and white rubbish. Removes the wilting flowers, and wipes over the side table. Then she gestures at the cold grey tea.

Would you like me to take this away?

Myra stares hard at the tea for several seconds, fighting tears.

I wanted lemons, she says helplessly. And begins to cry, without control, without hope. The woman puts down her cloth and reaches for the box of tissues.

Here, she says. It's OK. Take this, come on, it's OK.

Myra nods and weeps, and weeps.

Do you want me to find a nurse?

She shakes her head, and blows her nose.

Do you want me to leave?

She shakes her head again, and tries to apologise, but the sobs are huge.

The woman goes back to her cleaning trolley and puts the cloth and the spray carefully in their place. She puts a hand on the trolley and hesitates, then leaves it by the window and goes back over to the bed. She bends over the crying girl and touches her shoulder. Shall I get you lemons? she asks. Myra nods vigorously, still sobbing.

Tomorrow, OK?

Another nod.

Beautiful lemons. I promise. Stop crying now. Come on. Look, they've started the parade.

The two women stare up at the screen, where dizzying numbers of people swarm and then, very gradually, as the cameras lift and the scene is filmed from above, begin to snake around the museum. Myra watches through tears, and her sobs quieten. The building looks strange, like a relative who has been away a long time. Smaller. She looks at it dispassionately through the moving stream of faces and open mouths and waving hands. Neither woman thinks to turn the sound back on, and both are preoccupied, each looking for a particular face in the crowd.

37.

Three adults and a small child crouch at the edge of the bright pond. Sunlight falls from behind them and into the water, so that, for a foot or so at least, before the light is lost in the rich brown shadows, they can see all the way to the bottom. Theo shows them how to focus for different levels, from the skin of the water dancing with flies and the tiny hectic jewels of the whirligigs, to the yellowish shallows and their wriggling determined tadpoles, and in further and deeper to where slivers of fish hang momentarily and flick away; right down to the silt, which requires patience and a good eye, where ragged twigs and leaves lumber unexpectedly across the debris of their patch, camouflaged, like tanks. Diving beetles cut diagonals, like spaceships, between their heaven and their earth. Predatory white larvae wait, suspended, for whatever comes their way; others hang dormant halfway up the thick stems of plants which burst the surface into the clear air.

Dan has Teddy clutched firmly around the waist, and tries, by pointing and holding his head, to direct his gaze down to the fish in the middle water; but it is difficult to tell if he can actually see beyond the glitter of whirligigs on the surface, and the surface is all distraction in any case, with its yellow kingcups and its sunny reflections. At the far end of the pond, which is huge, more like a small lake, a pair of wild mallards skitter to a messy halt.

After a while Theo scoops out a couple of handfuls of fat black tadpoles and puts them in a washing-up bowl with a bit of duckweed. Lina persuades Teddy away from the water and together they sit and watch, with a shared fascination, their frantic wriggling. Theo, explaining as he goes in a long, low, monologue, shows Dan how to assemble a typical starter tank. Then he makes coffee for them all on a gas ring in the battered summerhouse. There are only two chairs, but it is sunny enough to sit on rocks. Teddy wanders between the adults with a biscuit in one hand and a stick in the other, and they talk over the top of his blond head, until it seems that he is determined to throw himself and his stick in the water. Lina holds out her arms and coaxes him to her.

I'll walk him round, she says.

Good idea; he might sleep after. You sure?

Quite sure. She smiles at them both, and sets off. They go back to their tank, load it onto the pick-up.

How many of these do you do in a week? asks Dan.

Depends on the time of year. We're busy enough right now. There are four more of these up at the house, I did them first thing.

And where are they going?

This lot? Um. Two primary schools, three private gardens, one day-care centre. And two unofficial stops.

Why unofficial? Dan is curious.

Not everything we do is done on request, or paid for.

Dan keeps quiet, waits to see if there is more to come, but Theo just grins at him, stands up and collects their mugs, looking absurdly tall inside the wooden house. As if he comes from a different century, thinks Dan.

You up for doing one more? Then we can go over to the trees.

Mud slips through his fingers like silk. It's the clay in it, Theo says, it's gorgeous stuff. Full of larvae. Dan's second tank takes far less time to prepare, and when he is done he gets up to stretch his back and wave at Lina and Teddy, now about three-quarters of their way around the pond.

There, he says. Looks good to me. Official or unofficial.

Theo looks at it critically. Bit short on the crowsfoot, he says; give it another clump.

Do they all take? asks Dan. I mean, you must have some that fail, don't get looked after properly; if there's a heatwave or something. He has a vision, from somewhere in his childhood, of a small green rancid pond.

Bound to lose a few, says Theo. But we help look after them once they're in, especially the schools. They have us over to help with lessons in the spring and summer. I've missed a few these last weeks, because of my mother; not everyone in the group is trained for schools.

Where are they? The others, I mean? Is this your head-quarters?

Yes, effectively; here and up at the house. The others are all over the place but you might meet a couple this after-noon. It depends how long you can stay.

That depends on Lina, says Dan. And the trains home.

If we're doing a drop this evening we can give you a lift, says Theo. I want to go in to the hospital in any case.

He walked all the way round! says Lina proudly. I helped him over the streams, that's all. Her trousers are wet at the hems, and there is mud on her tunic.

Bachgen mawr! says Dan, picking him up and hugging him.

We'll have some lunch at the house, shall we? says Theo. There's some bread and cheese. Apples. Then we can go over to the trees. I've got a couple to deliver for planting later on – you can help me dig them out.

But Lina is squatting down again at the edge, cupping water in her hands, letting it trickle through.

Is there a microscope at the house? she asks suddenly.

Yes. But there's one in there too.

Oh, she says. Could I? Just quickly?

Of course. I'll show you.

I'm taking him up to change his nappy, says Dan. See you up there, is that OK?

Go ahead. There's stuff in the fridge, help yourselves.

They go into the summerhouse and Theo reaches the microscope down from a shelf. Her fingers run over it softly. It's lovely, she says.

Pretty old-fashioned by now, he says. The one at the house is slightly better, but this isn't bad. Here, I'll get you a chair.

She makes a contented sound. I'm salt-water really, she says, but the water is so beautiful here. Thank you.

He watches her set up. What did you work on – in Syria, was it?

Yes. We were in Homs.

Oh, says Theo.

She looks up at his tone of voice, meets his gaze.

My brother was killed there, says Theo. Photographer.

She nods. My husband too, she says. Doctor.

She twists the lens into focus. Hey, this is busy water you have.

So what is your field?

She looks up again and smiles at him. Marine microbiology. Specifically, Radiolaria. More specifically, the actinota.

Ah, says Theo, delighted. Beautiful. Just beautiful. Have you seen the Blaschkas at the museum? The glass models?

I don't have much money, she says, apologetically.

You don't pay, says Theo. Amazingly. You can go and see them whenever you like.

93

38.

It's the underground, though she can't see the names properly. Not Paris, or Moscow, or Prague, or Madrid, just one of the grottier outer branches of the underground, on an unfamiliar line, with a familiar fear in her stomach. The carriage is packed at first, and she is standing, swaying, clutching the pole, keeping her eyes down as she always used to in case one day, by sheer ill luck, she should look straight up into the face of the man she is afraid of, but then the people begin to drain away and she is pretty much by herself, tucked against a window, watching indistinct platforms pull up, blur, and vanish. Between them she watches her own thin face stare back.

When the train stops and shudders and the harsh lights spring on she understands that it is time to get off, and steps onto a well-lit platform with no name and no one else around. There is only one exit, and she takes it, walking decisively in her smart shoes, click clack, along a corridor lined with bright posters advertising circuses, they all seem to be for circuses, three, four, five, half-a-dozen different circuses, which seems like a lot, though she hasn't got time to stop and look. Then the corridor splits without explaining why. She goes left. It is slightly darker here, and the posters are harder to catch in passing, but look to be much the same, if a little more tatty.

An escalator, going down, which seems counter-intuitive, but doesn't bother her any more than does the absence of other travellers. She stands on it, lets it carry her down gently past an elephant, a spangled girl, a dancing dog. There is another fork at the bottom, and this time she goes right, stepping onto one of those travelators that lets you walk and glide at the same time, like seven league boots. It sounds rattled, but goes fast enough to make her smile, she can't remember the last time she was on one of these. It pulls up at another junction. Left, now. She has a superb instinct for direction, though she knows it can be difficult for anyone underground.

After a good while walking like this her feet hurt. She takes off her shoes and puts them in her bag. The concrete feels cold through nylon tights, but not unpleasant, and, as the lights get dimmer and the posters on the wall are nothing but ragged coloured scraps, being practically barefoot means she can tell when the concrete runs out and the path becomes something like compacted soil, perhaps sand. It is obviously not any kind of approved official exit, but for some reason this doesn't worry her, and she is thinking quite phlegmatically that she could always retrace her steps and catch the next available train back when the path comes up against a stone wall. The light is very dim by now but she can see how massive the blocks are, and that they curve round; she can't make out how high they might go. There is a single low arched opening, like the entrance to a tunnel, through which she can see only dark.

She doesn't need to stoop, but does anyway. Her hands guide her through the vaulted archway, down some stone steps, three, four, five, and then she is on a circular terrace looking down on an enclosure, a shallow pit. There is an odour of straw and animals but what catches her breath is fresh air: she looks up to see stars, a million bright stars opening out above her in the night sky. She smiles, and as her eyes adjust to the new light, looks down.

On the floor of the pit a large figure is lying asleep. She can hear it breathing, and is curious enough to want to get closer. A zig-zag path leads her down into the enclosure. The figure is lying on a pile of straw and rags and as she moves quietly towards it she can see it is a man, or something like a man, naked and half-curled, his bull's head resting on one big arm. She is standing very close now and looks down on him, fast asleep, profoundly peaceful, and sees with fascination how at the nape of his neck, where the heavy animal head joins the big man's body, his dark hair is slightly tinged with grey. She stoops over and strokes him very gently. He moves, but doesn't wake.

Feeling suddenly exhausted by her long, long walk, and a little chilled in the starlight, she crouches down on the straw next to him and pushes herself into the space made by his curved warm body. Then she closes her eyes. The creature's big arm moves instinctively across her waist, and pulls her in tighter towards him.

39.

I tried a couple of days ago, she says, but I couldn't get through, I turned back. Stupid.

What happened? he asks.

Grief, she says. Loss. Hopeless. It didn't seem to matter any more, and then I didn't think about it at all until this morning. Then I saw you.

It's not just you, he says, don't worry. I've watched dozens of people turn back like that. The woman I know in Natural History says visitor numbers have been dreadful, and Dan says the university has set up some kind of cctv to record what happens. They interview people. They'll be after you, you watch.

She smiles. It didn't work, then, the Parade?

Apparently not. Come on, I'm here now, and going in anyway. I'll help you through.

He gives her his arm, and they climb the steps quickly. As they get nearer the top he puts his arm right around her shoulder and hurries her through. He doesn't let her go until they are in the main hall, under the echoing dome. He watches her look up, and around her, astonished.

I haven't been anywhere like this for a long time, she says. A long time. It's incredible.

Would you like some tea? he asks. I've got about twenty minutes before I'm expected. Or would you like me to show you the Blaschkas? Are you OK for time?

She nods and smiles. Early shift, she says. I'm finished for the day now. Tea would be good. Then I will explore all this. She makes a big gesture.

He laughs. Come on then.

She doesn't tell him that she hasn't eaten since breakfast at the hostel, many hours ago now; that the money for her cheese roll went on the lemons, carefully chosen and amicably haggled for at the corner shop. But she lets him buy her a thick slice of lemon cake, with almonds, and as the girl at the counter puts it onto a white plate she thinks of the three bright lemons left in a white hospital bowl this morning next to the sleeping girl. She imagines her waking.

They talk about their work, going almost straight into the finest details, discovering with pleasure how much of a shared language they possess. Her brown eyes are warm, and she tells him about being in the States as a young woman, an assistant researcher on a big international project on the Radiolaria. He tells her about articles he has seen, developments in the field she knows nothing about. They do not, not yet, talk about their dead.

Theo takes his leave; she has his phone number, she must ring him soon, he says. He points her towards Natural History. Past the stuffed animals and up the stairs, he says. Good luck.

Alone again, she feels daunted. She stands for a moment, a small figure in a dark tunic and headscarf, collecting herself beneath that huge ceiling, and then on an impulse heads up the grand flight of stairs to the right, to the art galleries.

There she drifts unsystematically, letting herself be drawn by colours, by faces, looking only occasionally at the labels. A handful of medieval Madonnas, each with Child. The women are lovely, though most of the babies are unconvincing, one or two almost grotesque; but she finds one she likes, a sweet-faced girl holding a boy who reminds her of Teddy, soft curly blond head, laughing. His mother must have been fair, she thinks; Dan is quite dark.

A large picture at the end of the room pulls her over. In the foreground is another Madonna, this one without Child, standing in front of a busy orchard full of workers piling fruit into wooden carts. She is tall, slender and stern. One hand holds a book close to her body; in the other is a glass of water, lifted to the light, a yellow September light which makes the orchard behind her glow. Lina is curious enough to read the label. *Our Lady of the Apple-Carts*, it says, *Italian, Tuscan School, possibly C15th*. Which leaves her none the wiser, really, but then her knowledge of Christian tradition, beyond the basics, is pretty weak. The woman looks almost unhappy, she thinks, in spite of the piles of beautiful apples, the assiduous peasants.

She moves on through other galleries. Castles, a whole wall of them, from all over Wales. Cardiff's looks lovely, she thinks, all trees and water where the road should be, and a man sitting in the dust with his dog; and a woman hanging out her washing to flap against the walls. Another room. Rodin's naked lovers unsettle her, and few of the Impressionists make her want to stop. She climbs a small flight of stairs to see where it goes, and finds a big wooden door with a sign on it: *Oriel Galatea Gallery : Closed / Ar Gau*. She comes back down a different way into a room full of modernist portraits, all of them apparently staring at her, and suddenly feeling she has had enough of Western tradition and its obsession with human form, hurries through two more rooms and down a short corridor to emerge, with relief, into a world of plants and creatures.

Five minutes later she has found the Blaschkas. The pictures she remembers seeing many years ago in a book do not come close. Inside the glass case, glass creatures, her creatures, a million times magnified, exquisite, strange and so familiar she cannot help the tears in her eyes. She blinks them away and circles the case in complete wonder. Reads blurrily how they were created by the Blaschkas, Leopold and Rudolf, father and son, in late nineteenth-century Bohemia, how their techniques have never since been reproduced. And there, centre-stage, is the *Actinota Heliosphaera*, the fretted glass sphere with irregular rays like slender spears of ice. Crystalline. Uncanny. More than ever, she thinks, more even than under the microscope, they look like entities from the farthest depths of space, from the stars; oh I wish you could see them Ali, can you see them? I wish you were here now, my husband, I wish you could see this.

And because she doesn't want to frighten the beautiful young man sitting discreetly against the wall in the attendant's chair, and because she is on the verge of something worse than tears, she hurries down the stairs, through the galleries, past groups of primary-school children in the busy main hall and out down the steps through the shiver of silence to find a bench where she can put her head in her hands and weep.

40.

Even if it didn't do any good, says someone, it didn't do any harm either; no harm at all.

Everyone, says Phoebe, had a wonderful time.

And it was good publicity, excellent really, with the professor's stunning media profile applications have simply rocketed up.

Luke, who has been told by someone very senior, in no uncertain terms, and in the strictest confidentiality, that he will be strongly recommended for fast-track promotion, is keeping modestly quiet.

Are there any biscuits? says someone.

Biscuits would be nice, says Phoebe. I'll go and ask. And has everyone got coffee who needs it?

Can you do me a fennel and liquorice tea? asks Aslan,

who is chairing this meeting in the professor's absence. There's a box by the kettle. *Wrth ymyl y degell. Diolch.*

They listen to three reports. The Museum Steps project now has a hundred and seventeen recorded negative reactions (NRs), and fifty-two follow-up interviews, mostly carried out by Phoebe who is very good at such things, and whose respondents offer a range of explanations for turning back. Roughly sixty-five percent say they felt an overwhelming sense of grief or despair, twenty-two per cent felt ill and dizzy, and the rest said they'd just thought of something else they needed to do instead, and had changed their minds.

The relevant graphs are projected and explored at some length. Luke presents a brief round-up of the benches project, though he explains that, because of involvement in the Parade, he has had to delegate most of the data-collection to other people. Everybody nods vigorously. The figures here speak for themselves, revealing a gradual, inexorable thinning of sitters, attributable mainly to the lower temperatures around the benches where the cold silence swirls and pools.

The third report, a PowerPoint prepared by the professor and presented by Aslan, shows the current reach and spread of the silence across the city. A month's worth of day-by-day mapping, with brief analysis of the directions of flow and the principal channels. A note at the end adds that they are currently in talks with Physics to explore ways of measuring the intensity, or it may be that the better word is viscosity, of the silence in different designated areas. This initiative meets with considerable approval.

The final item on the agenda is titled *Ar ôl yr Orymdaith/Post-Parade*. It asks for a brief assessment of the effect of the Parade on a) the silence and b) the profile of the university, and suggests, by way of concluding the meeting, a half-hour brainstorming session to come up with new ideas. The assessment part is quickly done, since the general feeling is that although the effect on a) was negligible, the effect on b) was entirely positive. The discussion that follows is predictably chaotic, with suggestions involving everything from electricity to hot-air balloons, and tempers are properly starting to fray when Aslan manages to remind them that the task in hand is not so much to solve the problem of the Interference – they have, after all, got most of the university science section on the case, quite apart from the work being done by the Government people and the scientists at the museum – as to be seen to be engaging with it in persuasively exciting ways.

Events, he says. Smaller-scale than the Parade, obviously, but public events, workshops, short films – things that will get reported in the media, to show we're doing our bit, you know they'll be bored with this story soon, we need to find ways of keeping it alive. Creative responses are always good, too. Can we find some artists?

41.

When he was about ten, on holiday, someone let him drive a tractor. Grey, a Massey Ferguson, and already very old, a thing of utter beauty. Later on, as a student, he would associate it at some odd subconscious level with that picture of Samuel Beckett, it was that important. Iconic. His hands on the wheel. And he feels like that now, sitting in the front of the van. Not driving, Theo is driving, but the effect is the same. His excitement is multiple and manifold: beautiful May evening; out without the baby; doing something new; something bordering on a misdemeanour. Theo understands, is pleased for him, amused.

And as they discuss the practicalities of the job in hand both men have glimpses of Lina sitting at the kitchen table in Dan's terraced house with half-a-dozen borrowed copies of the *NMBJ*, delighted to be catching up on work in her field again, but probably more delighted at the thought that she might be disturbed, he is teething again after all, and have to comfort him in her lap with warm milk and songs.

Dan has already done two ponds this last week, both commissioned, the first in a private garden, the second a home for the elderly, each time with Theo and a different member of the group. He finds them congenial company, these people, and he is full of admiration for their work. And they like him, clearly, enough to let him join a non-commissioned drop, which this evening will be on a roundabout somewhere on the edge of town. As they wait at some lights Theo points to one they did earlier, tucked between a disused factory and a bankrupt Bathroom Supply Stores. A little hawthorn tree, full of creamy blossom, guarding a small pond which throws back the pale grey of the empty warehouse as a circle of light.

How do you get away with it? When you're doing the digging, I mean.

You act as if you're supposed to be there; it's easy enough.

But don't people get suspicious? You lot lurking about on roundabouts?

We don't lurk. It's all very open. Hi-viz jackets, and a couple of flashy sponsorship boards, and a kind of weary expression as if you'd much rather be doing something else, and no one ever looks twice.

He glances sideways at Dan, then back at the road, straight-faced. You might need to work on your expression.

And when it's all done?

We leave a discreet sponsorship board up nearby; especially with roundabouts, everyone sponsors roundabouts. This Nature Initiative is Brought to You By...

And who sponsors you?

Theo snorts. No one. We make up acronyms, fancy logos. Occasionally for fun use a big name, Macdonalds, John Lewis, the Lottery. Or say it's something like a Council Partnership Initiative. In six, seven years of this no one has ever thought to think it might be otherwise.

They pull up at a bus stop to pick up a woman called Petra. She shoves a big plastic carry-all into the footwell and squeezes in beside Dan.

In fact, continues Theo, I've seen some of them quite pleased to take the credit; a couple of supportive letters to the local paper and they're convinced it was their idea all along. It's good all round.

Nice to meet you, says Petra.

My first non-commisioned, says Dan. I'm Dan.

Petra is a genius at designing fake logos, says Theo. She could be out there making millions in the real world, but no...

Wasting my talents on a bunch of guerrilla environmentalists, says Petra. How about you?

Me? says Dan. Oh, I'm here for the digging.

42.

Even before she wakes she can sense the change. The scent of them hangs in the air around her bed. There is no hurry to wake, the ebbing dream is not a difficult one, and coming out of it does not involve a struggle. When at last her eyes open the scent translates into an intensity of blue, a deep, impossible blue, hanging over her, and then very gradually into stems and bells, curved and nodding from the side-table, she thinks of seahorses, lying there looking up at them as if from the bottom of the ocean floor; she knows perfectly well by now not to try and come up too fast.

When at last she gets herself sat up in bed, and the sea-horses have resolved themselves into bluebells in a glass vase, she finds another gift: three bright lemons in a white bowl. The sun pouring into her white room makes the colours hyper-real, and they keep her entranced for several minutes. At last she reaches over and takes one of the lemons, holds it close to her face, smelling it, scoring it with her nails to get at the tang of the zest.

Theo walks in, makes an inarticulate noise and puts his hands over his face for protection. He peers through the cracks in his big fingers at a blur of red hair, bluebells and lemons in the sunlight and says she might have to put the fruit down, it's too much for him. She throws him the lemon; he catches it one-handed and sits on the end of the bed.

They're beautiful, she says, nodding at the flowers. Thank you. Are they from your place? From the pond?

Near enough, he says, just up and along a bit, and he describes the sloping hill across the marshy field, and the plantation with its rows and rows of whitebeam, service and rowan. We've got a kind of genetic spectrum going, he says, it's a museum project, they connect up, the trees, one species into the other. I'm the nursery for the different types; and I collect too. I helped find the Avon Gorge specimen, you know, the missing link...

She has no idea what he's talking about. How's the jelly stuff, the star-shot? she asks. Have you had any results?

He shakes his head. The bloke who was supposed to be doing the tests has been off work with depression for weeks. It's just sitting in the freezer, I imagine. Poor guy. I liked him; he was fun.

The thing, she says, the wall of silence – it's still there, isn't it? I mean, the Parade didn't make any difference did it?

It's still there, he says. He throws the lemon gently from palm to palm. Who brought you these? he asks. I know I didn't. Not that rather daunting colleague?

Myra pulls a face. Not her, no. There was a woman here, one of the cleaners. I was upset. It must have been her. I must have been asleep.

You were very asleep when I came earlier, he says. But you looked happy enough, for once. Do you think you're getting better?

The question is thrown out unthinkingly, almost off-hand, but as she glances up at him to answer they both re-alise that the answer matters, and not knowing what to say, she says nothing, just looks at him for a moment, and he at her.

Your mother? she asks, finally.

He can do that one. She's better and she's worse, he says; I knew it would be like this. There was a consultation this morning, that's why I came by quite early, and she's nearly fit enough to go home, as long as there's plenty of supervision – which will be me, mostly – and they reckon the leg is doing fine. She can get around with a frame thing, you know.

I know, says Myra sourly, they tried to give me one. I still managed to fall over.

You and gravity, he says, admiringly. That's a real thing you've got going between you.

Your mother, she says firmly, reaching out for the lemon. He places it gently in her hand, and keeps his hand cupped over hers for a second or two.

My mother. Well, the leg is OK but the head ... the mind ... is not. The consultation was supposed to begin the process of shifting, I mean transferring, the responsibility from the leg people to the mind people, only inevitably it's not that simple.

I can imagine. But does it mean she's going home?

I think so. Yes. I think so. Quite soon, I think.

Good.

Yes.

This time they avoid looking at each other. Theo holds out his hand again.

I take it you're planning to do more than just scratch and sniff at that poor lemon. Give it here. I'll get them to slice it up for you. Tea? Or in the water jug?

She narrows her eyes, contemplative. Both, she says. Both.

43.

The professor has timed a meeting in London so he can meet her at St Pancras, on her way back from Poland, or Italy, or Romania, from a conference or a performance, he forgets which. Stood against a wall he holds himself back, and watches the people flow past, their travelling faces looking ahead, fixed, absorbed. There are so many of them, all strangers, that the shock of her face feels like something more than just recognition. She spots him heading her way and gives him a brief, strong hug. He takes one of her bags and they find a cafe. It is full of people speaking different languages. They add theirs, silently, to the mix, their quick fingers sometimes tapping their keyboards, sometimes moving in the air. He finds more and more of her phrases coming back to him. He makes a few tentative moves of his own. This is her stubbornly idiosyncratic version of signing; a private language, a family language; the language in which she thinks best.

Their conversation is more subdued; they are both physically very tired. She from travelling, rehearsals and the intensity of the last performance; he from the job and its viciously multiplying demands. He tells her about the Parade, and some of its more peculiar effects – how if you stood in the right place the noise of a school choir, an opera singer, a brass band seemed abruptly swallowed up by the silence, as if they were all stepping into a giant invisible snake. But if you were in there, in with the rest, making a racket, you felt no real difference, you could hear everything; it was a bit chilly, that was all.

And nobody got hurt, he said. Amazing, really. And it kept the media happy, and the university came out of it very well.

But you still have the problem.

We do.

Do you, though, really? Is it getting worse? Or do you think it's found its level, this stuff?

I think it has slowed down a bit. But I'd say on balance it's getting worse. Slowly.

Plan?

No plan.

She shivers, and shrugs, and they look at each other, thinking of the castle.

Been on your shooting weekend yet? she asks.

Not the season, darling. Shoot damn all in May; I had a look. Roebuck and rabbits. It'll be August, I imagine, the glorious twelfth or thereafter, Jesus Christ.

You'll look fantastic in tweeds. Don't fret.

He pulls a face at her.

August is pretty late, she says, ticking off the weeks on her fingers. Another week of May, June, July. If it is getting worse, as you say, you need to try something before then. That is, if you think the silence really is a problem – you all seem to be managing fine at the university, don't you? And I don't see much fuss about it in the media by now, everyone just seems to have got used to it. Who's actually getting hurt?

Homeless people, he says; mad people, the people who sit on benches. No one with any influence. Some small businesses, whose customers have just given up. Wifi and mobile signals not exactly screwed up, but jittery, right across the city. That might stir someone, eventually, but you're right, no one's complaining much now, after the initial flurry. Um, who else. Employees at the museum, depressed. Visitor numbers down – though I imagine they might have done quite well out of the publicity for the Parade. But I think it will get bad again soon; this feel-good thing is probably a bit of a mirage, a blip...

She raises her eyebrows and laughs at him. Now there's a surprise, she says; and you the marketing experts and all.

Don't start, he says. Don't start all that. You have no idea how quaint you sound. You lost that battle years ago. Give up.

There is a small stirring of flame in her eyes, and her hands start to quicken. He grabs one in mid-air and holds it tight. Now he looks straight at her, speaking aloud.

Not now, Meg, he says. And not me. Listen, come on, I'm asking for your help, not another critique of a bloody system you abandoned and I didn't. It is slow, like I said, this stuff, but it is ultimately corrosive, and you've felt for yourself that it's not going to do any of us any good. So tell me, *cariad*: what happens next? What are we going to do?

44.

Rowndarowndarownd, says Teddy.

Mmm, says Dan, reading small ads in a local paper left tactically on a plastic chair. Rowndarrownd.

It's drizzling, and the wash has fifteen minutes to go, and it's not worth the hassle, he thinks, going out again and coming back. And besides, he has his eye on the best dryer, full of someone else's clothes but due to stop in twelve minutes. Eleven.

Rowndarownd, Rowndarownd, sings Teddy, crouched in admiration in front of the machine and making circles with his hands.

All day long, says Dan. And most of them yours, he thinks, I hardly have any clothes to my name, and look at you, three bags full. The mothers pass stuff on, he hardly ever has to buy things: the little vests and the all-in-one pyjamas and the smart coats. The fiddly dungarees and the stripy tops. Jumpers with embroidered tractors. He deselects the ones with unsuitable slogans: *Mummy's Little Helper; If You Think I'm Cute You Should See My Dad*. And all the Disney ones, unless they're seriously retro and make him feel nostalgic. And all the sub-military ones, the khaki, helmets, guns. And this morning already, feeling unusually

111

purposeful, he has sorted out all the clothes that are suddenly much too small, and stuffed them into bags with the pile of deselected items, and taken them, balanced dangerously on the hood of the buggy, to a charity shop en route for the launderette. The week's wash is in a rucksack on his back. He feels superbly organised.

Three minutes. It's Saturday, but early, and the launderette is fairly quiet. No one else is staying, they all have shopping to do. Not having money, Dan tries increasingly to avoid shops. But because it is Saturday, he thinks after a while, Luke might not have meetings. He texts him: What are you up to today?

Buying socks.

When?

Now.

Nice. He almost adds, buy some for me, but doesn't trust Luke not to take him seriously and start asking for shoe sizes. Mind you, he badly needs socks.

You?

Launderette near the station. Washing socks.

By night, he thinks, but doesn't write that either, *all seated on the ground*.

Cool, I'll come by, texts Luke.

Cool, returns Dan, with a grin, and then says it aloud to Teddy: Cool.

Rowndarowndarownd, says Teddy, concentrating hard.

Not any more, says Dan. It's finished.

They have just stuffed all the wet clothes into the top dryer when Luke appears, clutching a small M&S bag and looking pleased to find them.

All done, he says, waving the bag vaguely in the air.

Last of the big spenders, says Dan gravely. And it's not

even ten yet.

Have you, ah, had breakfast? asks Luke.

Not as such. Good idea.

Luke treats them to croissants and frothy coffee and warm milk, and tells them the latest university news, though he is tactful enough not to mention his suddenly shining prospects. He is just explaining one of the new schemes for tackling the silence when Dan's phone rings, making them both jump.

It can't be you, says Dan, fumbling in a pocket, so who the hell...

It's Theo, sounding far away and unusually riled.

I need that Californian man, he says, the one with the iPad. Have you got his number? I need to speak to him right now.

Dan passes the phone to Luke.

It's for you, he says.

45.

He crosses the main road, through a channel of silence which cuts out the beeps of the green man at the crossing, and enters the Gorsedd gardens, bright with flower beds. He has about an hour and a half before the meeting with the consultants, and he wants to get a coffee and check something quickly in the herbarium at the museum. He feels in his pocket for the notebook with the rowan leaves pressed neatly inside. He doesn't notice the man until he is almost upon him. The man is holding a paintbrush and standing thoughtfully in front of Myra's bench looking at three large cans of paint. A camera on a tripod is filming him looking thoughtful.

Theo takes in the scene, and stops.

What are you doing? he asks.

The man, who is young and Asian, with spiky blond hair, pale jeans and a black t-shirt, beams at him.

I'm glad you asked me that, he says, glancing at the camera.

Theo waits. The young man continues to stare intensely at his cans of paint.

So? says Theo. What are you doing?

I'm an artist, says the man.

OK.

And I'm Responding to the Interference.

OK. How? You're not using this bench, are you?

The artist looks delighted. I am! he says. I'm going to paint it three different colours. One after the other, not all at once. It's quick-drying paint.

No, says Theo. But the young man is away. I'm going to paint it white first; then red; then grey. Or possibly black; I have another pot over there, look. Do you know why?

No ... says Theo, meaning something else entirely. No, you...

Because, says the man happily, white will represent the cold, enigmatic world of the silence. Then red will represent the profound human struggle against it, and then grey, or possibly black, will be the overwhelming sense of despair that it induces ... a sort of total alienation. I think, you know, I think probably the grey.

No, says Theo, more decisively, moving round to face him properly ... you can't...

And, says the young man, I should actually have started half an hour ago, but the stupid thing is, you know, I can't decide which *order* to do the colours in, whether to start with the white, the problem itself, or whether to end up there. Basically, I can't decide on the *narrative*. He points the paintbrush at Theo. What do you think?

I think, says Theo firmly, that you shouldn't touch that particular bench. I think you should leave it alone.

The artist gives him a lovely smile and shakes his head. No, he says, it's got to be this one, see, with the museum behind it. Look, stand here, you'll see what I mean. See? I'm going to splice in clips of the Parade – it's a film, the artwork is a film, of me painting the bench – and then some of the cctv shots of people turning back in despair. And bits from the interviews after. See?

Are you from the University?

Mm. Well, I'm an Independent Artist, obviously, but yes, they commissioned me for the Artistic Responses Project.

OK, says Theo. I do understand. But not this bench, I'm sorry. He deliberately moves the cans of paint onto the ground, and sits down on the bench with his arms folded.

The young man looks baffled. But it was this one in my project proposal, he says. I don't see how it could be any-where else.

Try the castle, says Theo. The castle's the problem, not here.

But the footage... He is very disconcerted by now.

No, says Theo, and spreads out his long arms like wings along the top of the bench. *No.*

The artist pulls himself up to his full height, suddenly very dignified and stiff.

I don't think you have the right to stop me in any case. It's all cleared with the council, so you can't be from them. Who are you, anyway?

Theo just shakes his head and sits firm.

The man fumbles for his phone and starts jabbing for names and numbers. The office is shut on Saturdays, but Phoebe said anytime he needed her. He gets a wrong number, and tries again. Theo listens to him tripping over his own tongue, outraged and not terribly coherent, and wonders if he will miss the hospital appointment, and whether he should phone to tell them; and how long he might be prepared to sit on the bench, and under what kind of duress. It has started to drizzle a bit, which might put a halt to the painting for today anyway. Then he remembers Luke, and he too reaches for his phone.

46.

Elin from work has been and gone, with a pretty tin of homemade biscuits and disquieting news. At least, it should be disquieting, she thinks, carefully extracting two of the biscuits and rearranging the rest, pressing the lid back on tight. But it feels like news from a long way away, news from nowhere that matters, though of course it should matter, rumours of redundancies, and you-know-who making sorrowful comments in meetings about expensive sick-pay arrangements when healthy hard-working staff are in danger of losing their jobs.

And yes, Elin will admit she is worried, because she and Tony want to start a family, please don't tell anyone, and she knows that maternity leave, like illness, is a wedge in the door, that you may never get your hours back to what they were, that sometimes you don't get your old job back, you get landed with stuff way down the payscale, or indeed you don't get any kind of job back at all. Bonny Elin, funny Elin, tired and anxious. Don't worry, said Myra, reassuring, they know they can't cope without you, you'll be fine, you go ahead and have that baby, that's what matters, don't let them stop you. And Elin had looked at her then with a kind of dawning despair, and taken her hand and cried a bit and said she was sorry for being so thoughtless, so selfish. No, said Myra, come on now, I'm fine; don't you be so daft.

Now she looks sleepily at the last half-lemon in the bowl near her bed, and thinks with satisfaction that she has something appropriate to give the woman in return. Biscuits are better than bluebells, as presents, especially when the bluebells are drooping a little, as hers are by now. She had come again this morning, after missing a couple of days, and had been pleased to find Myra sitting up drinking tea. That's better, she said. Those lemons are working.

They are, said Myra. I can feel a difference.

I'll bring you more, then, said the woman, if that's the last one.

Oh you mustn't, said Myra. I mean, I love them, they're beautiful, but you mustn't put yourself out. Here – let me give you some money for them, at least...

But of course when she had looked in her handbag and found her purse she had no real money, just coppers and useless cards. She hasn't needed money for so long that the whole idea of payment felt elaborate and awkward. She was perplexed, but the woman just smiled at her, pulled off one of her rubber gloves, and raised a worn index finger with a blue stone ring.

I'll bring one, she said. Just one. Fine?

Fine, said Myra. Thank you, very much.

You get well, said the woman, and trundled her cleaning trolley off down the corridor.

She had read for while then, one of Theo's odd books, and learned that *Genesistrine is a region in the Super Sargasso Sea, and that parts of the Super Sargasso Sea have rhythms of susceptibility to this earth's attraction.* She likes that. Rhythms of susceptibility. She thinks she probably has them herself. And then the new consultant had arrived, a fierce, likeable Scottish woman, to discuss the options for dealing with the symptoms of post-operative early-onset menopause, the possible ways of holding it at bay, so that she wouldn't be thrown from girlhood, or young womanhood, straight into a fragile and osteoporous old age, her bones as light and brittle as a bird, her hair dry and thinning. It's thinning anyway, she'd pointed out, from the chemo. I know, the consultant said, but it should come back. And then the nurse had taken her blood-pressure and decided that it might be edging a little closer to Normal. It's the lemons, Myra had explained, drowsily. They seem to be working. And they had agreed with her about the lemons, and left her to sleep.

The sleep was interrupted by Elin, who stayed for half an hour or so. It reclaimed her afterwards, not a deep sleep, this time, and its dreams were not dramatic, but fragments of them clung to her as she drifted in and out. Sitting on the lower steps of the building in a summer frock, in the sun, she was holding a creature in her lap, short brownish-grey fur, trembling, not a cat, not a dog, she'd never been keen on dogs. Possibly an aardvark, but she suspected not, she'd have remembered the snout. Holding it safe until the building was ready for it, and could send someone out to collect it.

She is woken at last by Theo, out of breath and in a state.

Two minutes, he gasps. No, one, bugger. Appointment downstairs. No time. Just wanted to tell you I saved your bench from a terrible fate, thought you'd be pleased. Explain later.

He hurries over and kisses her on the top of her head. She hands him a biscuit.

I must have known, she says. Look, I saved you this, as a reward.

47.

When she is settled and dozing in the big green chair he walks down to the pond for ten minutes of fresh air, hoping she will not wake and be at a loss without him. He feels vaguely guilty for going out at all, but he has to get out, because his head hurts and because although it has only been a matter of weeks since she had the accident he is now not used to having another person at home, not this person; it is not like before. She is so fragile and so confused he cannot see how they can possibly avoid it happening all over again, and worse this time, the fall, the white hospital, the distances in her eyes increasing. She had looked out of the taxi window all the way home. He held her hand. Every few minutes she turned to him with questions she could not formulate and a nervous smile that struck his heart. He had told her the names of places as they passed through them.

Standing now by the pond's edge staring down he could swear the horsetails have grown an inch since this morning. Weird things, their perpendicular spears pushing through the water into air; they are just beginning to branch out. Underwater, in that other world, a few of the stems are thick with feeding tadpoles, sticking like iron filings to a thin magnetic rod. Like living chimney-brushes, wriggling totem-poles; tad-poles. He wonders why only two or three stems get chosen for the feast. Crouching down to get a better look his eyes are drawn further in, to the sticklebacks hanging, waiting, flicking away. Little hunters, their sky-blue and salmon colours just beginning to intensify. A pale worm thrashes suddenly into view in the mud at the bottom; it looks as if it is being harried, hunted down by a handful of small fish.

A swift dives across him into a cloud of tiny dancing flies. He straightens up, and the headache returns magnified. He looks across the marshy land towards the hills with a new kind of apprehension, at June buttercups too bright and shiny in the heavy air, at dark green rushes somehow loaded with obscure significance. Only without remembering, without noticing in the first place, could anyone ever assume that early summer must be infallibly lovely. We forget days like these. The air is yellowish, thick with the gathering dead.

The last time the three of them had sat down together for a meal must have been nearly ten years ago, her seventieth, she hadn't wanted to go out. They'd all cooked, all at once, different dishes, chopping and frying across each other, drinking wine and beer, dancing round her, teasing, playing the fool. They'd dug out stories for her then, from when they were small, glimpses of games and worlds she was not party to, but whose contexts she remembered far better than they could. Nothing was said about work until after she had gone up to bed, and the two of them sat drinking and talking at the kitchen table. A discussion that got heated. A sheaf of photos thrown down like a gauntlet: figures and faces and buildings. Drunk and frightened and filled with righteous anger, his brother had made him look, and look properly, at every single one. *You don't have to go back,* said Theo. *You've done enough.* And his brother had put his weary drunken head down on the table and said nothing more.

The pictures survived, he thinks, though the photographer had not. They must be in the attic up at the big house somewhere, tucked in a file with all the boxes of stuff. He wonders how Lina got on with the Blaschkas. And then, suddenly stronger and more determined, he turns to walk back up to the cottage, concerned she might have woken, and ready to face the new world indoors. But while his back was turned the evening light has taken sudden hold of swathes of red sorrel lining the path up to the house, and now it flings the colour at him; it is the colour of Myra's hair, and it hurts.

48.

One by one, in a street curving down from near the castle, like lights going out, like teeth falling out, over two or three months, shops have been closing down. They haven't gone like falling dominos, one neatly after the next; just more and more gaps appearing until there are more gaps than teeth. His landlady's shop, the hairdressers, is among them. People just stopped coming, she said. Even the old ladies. Like they'd all died or something. And the students, they used to come; we were reasonably priced, see. I don't know what's happened. It's a mess, it is.

So the rent has gone up, sharply, and Dan is looking everywhere he can think of for a new home. Two adverts in the launderette came to nothing. The property rental people make no attempt to hide their opinion that a toddler is a liability. I can't get rid of him, though, can I? says Dan, trying to be reasonable, and the girl just shrugs and says it doesn't help. Pushing the buggy out into the bright sun he eyes up the distance from the agency to the gaping row. It won't be long, he thinks. It's heading your way. You should have been more sympathetic.

He wavers between the park and the library. He needs the internet to trawl for accommodation, and he needs his fix of stars. But it is a beautiful summery day and Teddy shows no signs of needing a nap, and while he still has his swipe card and free access he feels he should make the most of it. They pass Lina's bench, and he wonders how she is; wonders where she is. Up at the hospital, no doubt. He could always ask her about getting a cleaning job there, when his money runs out, since having a PhD doesn't seem to be a handicap. Or maybe she just didn't tell them. He hopes that she will want to fix up another session of babysitting soon, so that she can look after Teddy and he can go out again on a drop with Theo. But he cannot remember how to get hold of her, there was, she said, some problem with her phone.

When they reach the animal wall Dan gets Teddy out of the buggy and lifts him up onto his shoulders. Small hands grab his hair and pull. Stop it, you menace, he says; don't tug like that. He holds both of the child's feet together with one hand, and steers the empty buggy expertly along the pavement with other; they count the blackened animals along from right to left, making, where possible, the appropriate noises until a tiger-roar cuts out like engine stalling, and Dan hurries them through a slice of silence, and in through the gate. He lifts the boy down from his shoulders and sets him loose to run in zigzags across the grass. He guesses they are probably heading for the climbing tree, with its thick low branches grazing the lawn. But a flash of yellow up behind the castle distracts them both. There are diggers. They go and investigate, *digger* being one of Teddy's few but powerful words, and diggers in action counting as high entertainment for them both.

The job is just beginning, and seems to involve, as far as he can make out from a complicated information panel, shoring up the eroded banks of the leat behind the castle and hooking the water away back down to the river somewhere near the bridge. *Shoring up these fragments*, he thinks, automatically. *Shoring up these fragments against*. One of the guys in orange grins and waves at them. Teddy looks up at Dan, delighted, and for the first time, completely, he sees Jane smile.

It gets cold, watching the diggers, and after a while he chases Teddy back down towards the bright flowerbeds and the friendly curving tree. He sits on the horizontal trunk and watches the child climb like an inexperienced koala. The smile flickers in his head like the fragment of a song.

So many ways   that we   don't die.

49.

Stinks in here, says the thin girl in the vest. I only came in for a cup of tea, not a fuckin curry, not for breakfast, Jesus, who has curry for breakfast?

Lina keeps on frying; onion, garlic, cardamom, spices. It is best not to apologise. It is best not to say anything at all.

I'm sorry, she says, quietly, without looking up. I'm cooking supper now because it will be late when I get in. I won't be long.

The girl pushes past her, fills the kettle, puts it on. Fuckin stinks it does, she says to herself as much as anyone, I only came in for a cup of tea.

Lina pulls the rings on a can of tomatoes, a can of chick-peas, and adds them to the pan. She says nothing more. The girl makes her tea and sits up on the bar stool by the counter. She gets her phone out of her jeans, swears at it, puts it back. She heaps sugar into her tea and stirs it, then waves the spoon at Lina's back; the scars run like tiger claw-marks, like glacial striation, up the inside of her thin white arms to the crook of the elbow.

You need to get out, she says, not threatening, not vicious, just matter of fact. Jen and some of the others been saying it, and now there's two more coming in this weekend. Not because you're a paki, it's just there's no room, see. These new girls need more help; you got a job. And no one's beating the shit out of you. You need to get out you do. Make us all some room.

Lina stirs the contents of the pan to stop it sticking. The idea of a sprig of fresh coriander flits through her head. The idea of her sister stirring something similar, but for a larger number of people, somewhere in Palestine, flits through her head. It would have been better, she thinks, if it could simmer for ten more minutes, much better, to have it quietly simmering there while she did a few jobs round the tiny kitchen. But she turns off the ring, and tips everything, much too hot, into a plastic bowl. She washes and dries the pan, puts a lid on the plastic bowl, and opens the fridge.

Don't put it near my stuff, says the girl. Stinks, it does.

Lina rearranges the food on the crowded top shelf but her bowl still won't fit. She pulls out some items from the back, a half-eaten meat pie rimed with white mould; a chocolate dessert two months out of date, a bag of rancid salad, and puts them carefully on the counter.

These are old, she says. Do you think it's OK to throw them out?

The girl shrugs, suddenly not interested. She is looking at her phone again and seems better pleased this time. Lina puts the food in the bin, and her bowl in the fridge, and leaves her to her tea and her texts.

50.

He has moved things around to make it easier for her during the day, when he is out. Almost everything she needs is in the big kitchen where they eat; the green chair for sleeping and reading, books and magazines and the radio beside it on a shelf. And he has moved the cherrywood table and the curved oak chair from the sitting room, now her bedroom, and placed them under the bay window, looking down through the fruit trees in the garden and over the fields towards the pond, a glimmer in the distance. He can't tell if her eyes can translate the glimmer into water any more, but it makes him feel better to think of her occasionally looking up from her strange drawings towards his place of work.

He doesn't think the rearrangement has been too confusing, and he likes the room this way. He has removed some chairs and a good deal of clutter, it feels more spacious, brighter. Important familiar objects are still in place: pictures and photographs and plates, a worked blanket, a grey stoneware jug. Her clay figures. But the dining table is cleared of its toppling piles of books and papers; he has moved most of them upstairs into one of the bedrooms. Every time he leaves the house he turns the switch on the electric oven off, and gags it with thick black tape; he turns the gas hob off at the canisters outside. He has hidden the iron. Not that he ever uses it, himself, but she might take it into her head to start ironing teatowels or something. His mind is full of possibilities, as if he were the parent of a small child, constantly playing through dreadful scenarios.

He brings flowers back indoors from the field and the woods and the garden. Frothing meadowsweet and sharp dark irises; buttercups and sorrel. She has everything, he hopes, to keep her content in that downstairs space, to stop her wandering up and down, where she could fall, to stop her going into the garden without him and forgetting how to get back in, heading off down the lane perhaps, towards the big road. He thinks of stair-gates, as for a toddler; of an electronic tagging system, a sort of invisible tripwire, as for a low-security prisoner. He thinks of an impenetrable circle of thorns and roses, as for a sleeping princess. And then he thinks that if the silence had got into the valley, and noosed itself around their house, as it had around the museum, around the benches, around the park, it might have kept her in, stopped her drifting – she has always hated to be cold. But the silence is nowhere near them, and never likely to come seeping up their way; the hills, he thinks, will keep us safe.

The first few days were difficult. He felt he could not leave her for more than half an hour at a time. He cancelled or delegated all his jobs for the week, and carried the image of Myra's white room around in his head like an awful shrine. He gave his mother music, classical, soothing; and the stuff she'd always liked, Dylan, Joni, the old blues guys, both of them singing along. He left magazines and newspapers for her to flip through. He cooked as he had always done in the evenings, and represented his brother and his father in increasingly surreal, often lively conversations across the crumpled folds of space and time. When she was deep in one of these discussions she could do things without thinking – dry dishes, sweep up, sort clothes.

Then he found paper in a cupboard upstairs. Big sheets, thick paper, and bundles of pencils, all the Hs, all the Bs, and charcoals, their perfect points untouched. He carried it all downstairs and laid it out for her under the bay window.

Draw something, Mam, he said. I'm going to work now. Draw something for when I get back.

51.

After seven days of waiting, and with doctors and nurses seeming to come round less and less often, Myra decides she must learn to walk. She has managed for quite a while now to get over to the ensuite toilet in the corner of her room by first sliding into the chair, resting, and then working her way slowly, head-down, along the windowsill, refusing to make eye-contact with the huge gull looking in sideways at her. But that is all compromise, she thinks. Almost as bad, though not quite, as slithering across the floor on your belly. She must get vertical, and on her own, since no one appears inclined to help.

She wonders, now, if she had had a phone that worked, and if she had given him her number, whether they might have talked, or texted. But the dead thing in her handbag has long since lost the power to connect with the very few numbers stored inside it: Elin, her mother, no longer answering, a cousin and two old schoolfriends, the secretary at work and the doctor. Since she came back from London she has had no email account outside work, has never been on any kind of social network, and never shopped online; she has made herself as light and as invisible as humanly possible, at least without being some kind of spy or criminal. All she had wanted then was to not be found; now she is not so sure. It all depends, she supposes, who finds you first.

They had left the zimmer-frame. She wakes one afternoon and stares it down coolly for a while; then she slides into her chair and sets off round the windowsill as usual. But on her return she lets go of the edge and grasps the light metal instead. Keeping her head down to cheat gravity, and taking one step at a time, she gets about half-way back before the dark tide comes rushing in; she summons just enough strength to stumble forward and pitch onto the bed. It's a start.

So one morning when Lina comes in pushing her cleaning trolley she finds herself face to face with Myra, pale as porcelain, pushing her metal frame. They look at each other for a long moment, and then Myra says, very slowly, if you make me laugh, or cry, I will probably fall over. Also, I think I'm stuck. Lina nods, carefully expressionless, and comes over with a hand outstretched. Let go of the frame, she says, you can walk to the bed with me, look. Myra is breathing quickly, like a cat, and her eyes are narrowed in concentration.

Come.

There is more strength in hands, even small hands, thinks Myra, than in metal frames. Holding Lina's, she makes it to the bed, and lies flat for a minute or so to keep the darkness at bay, before raising herself on her pillows and gesturing for Lina to sit on the bed beside her.

Thank you, she says, I really was stuck.

Lina smiles and strokes the white hand, then sighs and shakes her head and gets to her feet. I have to get on with this, she says, I'm running late. They'll be round to check up on me soon, it's a quality audit morning. They'll be round this way.

Just empty the bin, says Myra, the room's perfectly fine. I'm really sorry to have made you late.

Lina stands with one hand on the trolley and tries to smile. But after last night, the kindness is too much, it breaches her.

When I got back to the hostel, where I stay, last night, she says. When I got back, the food I had prepared in the morning, the food in the fridge, it was all over the kitchen, thrown around, in the sink, on the walls, on the sides, on the floor, it was everywhere, it took a long time to clean up, an hour, maybe more. They want me to leave. I am taking up space. Because nobody is beating the shit out of me, the girl said; I have to make room.

Myra has wrapped her arms tight round her knees, and her face is full of pain. What will you do? she asks. What will happen tonight?

Lina shrugs, shakes her head, and reaches for the bin-liner in her trolley. It will be fine, she says. You get well. You get well now.

But Myra is sliding off the bed again trying to get at the bag in her locker. She fumbles the zip and roots around inside. Pulls out keys.

My flat, she says, waving them. My flat. Come back after your shift and I'll tell you how to get there. The fridge might be horrible. But it's nice enough, the place. There used to be a little orange tree, I can't remember if I asked Elin ... no, ah no, I'm afraid it's probably dead.

52.

Dan stares with a kind of inert fascination over the railings. The huge rectangle of filthy water stretches down towards the Bay, dark even under a bright blue sky. Teddy is crouched at his feet, an arm wrapped round one of his legs, peering through the railings at the extraordinary mess of green slime and thick brown water, and a constellation of crisp packets, cans, a plastic shoe, a messageless bottle. A viscous, milky turquoise stain has spread across the surface like the map of an impossible country; the air is hot and still, and no breeze alters its coastline or shifts its borders. Unbelievably, there are four or five birds; coots with white-stripe heads, clucking and squealing, and two exotic-looking grebe things, paddling around in the slime and occasionally meeting, courteously enough, head to head. Teddy is watching them, and calls out to them softly, *dak-dak*, but Dan is fixated by the poisonous-looking blue stuff, which doesn't, quite, look enough like paint; he finds himself perversely hoping that it isn't some kind of algae, that it would be too horrible to think of it blooming naturally, brought into being in heavy heat and powerful light from that thick evil soup of ingredients. Theo would know, he thinks, but christ could even Theo redeem this place? How do the birds manage, he wonders. Perhaps there are poisonous-coloured slugs in there for them to feed on; or deadly bright-blue frogs like in South America.

Last month, before this thick heat took hold, they had been out at Theo's place, working, with Lina; and Teddy, being that much closer to the ground, had spotted them first: dozens and dozens of tiny, perfect frogs, clambering through the grass at the edge of the pond as if it were a jungle. Once you started looking the whole path was alive with them, heading with equal determination in different directions. Lina had caught one to show Teddy, close up; the size of a fingernail, absolutely perfect. *Broga*, said Dan;

and Teddy had echoed him: *Brog*. Theo was as pleased as a child. *Not one instance have we, he declaimed, of tadpoles that have fallen to this earth. Never has a fall of adult frogs been reported... Always frogs a few months old...*Then he had gone into the summerhouse and come out with a brown leather book, and read to them, like a preacher, the lesson of the day:

As soon as the frogs are released from their tadpole state, they immediately take to land; and if the weather has been hot, and there fall any refreshing showers, you may see the ground for a considerable space perfectly blackened by myriads of these animalcules, seeking for some secure lurking places.

Dan can feel the empty buildings behind him, gaping, and he reaches down to touch Teddy's silky blond head. No brogs here, he says; come on. Even if the tip-off had been right, he thinks, and this had been a secure lurking place, he couldn't have faced this every morning. And imagine the bleakness in winter. The JCB man, the one who had waved up by the castle, and had recognised them when they came past again afterwards, and had lifted Teddy up into the cab, Rick, or Rhod, he said his name was, had told him about some deal down at the wharf, in what was possibly the last office left, he thought, where they were renting out empty space sort of under the radar, not quite illegal, but not quite legitimate, and god knows there's enough empty space down there. But the office, when he'd found it just now, was as dead as the rest of them. He could see through the windows that nothing had happened there for months. Ghost offices full of the languishing souls of defunct estate agents, solicitors, data-information-solutions-providers, clustering round their dried up water-coolers, desperate for some news.

Dan unclasps Teddy from his leg and takes his hand; they leave the buggy and walk down the long edge of the rectangle. He notices more turquoise blotches in the water; to their right, where the offices stop, is a rampant tangle of buddleia and yellow ragwort, of yarrow and cow parsley and thistle. The buddleia is thick with butterflies, heady, sickly sweet, and he remembers, as he always does, that scene from the French book they did at school, at A-level, a scene where the butterflies feast on the corpses under a piti-less provençal sun. He is about to turn back when he sees a figure heading towards them from the direction of the bay. A man in a pale-grey suit and white shirt, slight, trim, walking quickly, with a briefcase slung over his shoulder and a phone in one hand. There is something familiar about him, thinks Dan, as he gets closer; he must be a politician, a newsreader, a face from the papers. When the man is very close he sees who it is, the professor, Luke's professor, in-deed, briefly, his own head of department, in the first months of that failed post-doc project. He does not expect recognition, and doesn't get it, but the two men do look at each other as they pass, and exchange a civil hello. Dan waits a moment by the railings before turning round; he doesn't want to seem to be following, but nor can he bear this place very much longer. The professor has disap-peared. He lifts the child up onto his shoulders and quickens his own steps back.

53.

He has to walk. The conference room down at the Bay was comfortable, and nicely air-conditioned; the iced water had sprigs of fresh mint in it, there was room for everyone at the meeting to breathe, the coffee was drinkable and the Powerpoint worked beautifully, but as he picks his way through the car parks and the slip roads he knows that the heat of the sun and the thick warm air in his face are infinitely less suffocating than all that. He badly wants to phone her, to talk at once, immediately, voice to voice, and that, of course, is the one thing he cannot do. His slim fingers cannot text quickly enough.

Where are you? *Angen siarad*. This week?

The answer, when it comes, is laconic:

Cneifio.

Damn, he thinks, bloody mountain sheep. Everyone else is long done by now, christ, it's practically autumn, they'll be freezing by next week, poor buggers, cold and shivering up on the crags.

Angen siarad! he replies, put out.

Du calme, du calme, she says; write to me later, send me the gist.

He wonders, then, as he reaches the big rectangular water, how one might ever convey the gist of such a meeting, with so many interested parties, himself included, trying to control not merely the narrative, but the sub-plots, the subtexts, and a whole greyish spectrum of barely acknowledged meanings, a tangle of intentions and agendas, most of them as invisible as they were unpleasant. He had been asked to give a presentation on the current state of the silence to a dozen or so representatives of the power of the city: to the man from the Council, ill-prepared and out of his depth, the rival VCs, the two enigmatic women from the Corporation, the personable bloke from the BBC and at least three – four? – people working for ButeCo, though all were ostensibly independent and representing something else: the Parks and Gardens Charitable Foundation, the Dock Development Group, and the more nebulous Super-markets Consortium. The gist, he supposes, if there was a gist, was that several of the more powerful members of his audience had not much liked his maps, or had not, rather, liked the obvious conclusion to be drawn from them, and that the entire four-hour meeting had managed, astonishingly, to avoid mentioning the castle. They had made encouraging noises about supporting future research; ButeCo, indeed, would be delighted to provide immediate funds to help resolve the wifi issues. But the bottom line, apparently, was that the silence was nobody's responsibility, and not enough of a problem for any of them to need to act. Even his own VC, thoroughly briefed and entirely, he thought, committed to pushing for some kind of action, had simply sipped her water quietly, looking anxious and saying nothing. He wonders now, in anger and frustration, what the deal was, in the meeting that must have happened before the meeting, between the very select few.

Cneifio, in the name of heaven! Bloody mountain sheep.

He passes a young man with dark hair holding a little boy up to look over the railings at the rancid water. He nods and says hello. Then he turns abruptly off and crosses an empty road, picking a zig-zag path through intersecting water-channels connecting an incongruous suburban residential area to the groups of surviving businesses clustered around their car-parks. It feels like a different route every time, he thinks; the bridges move, new channels open up. The walking has helped, and he pays more attention, now, to his surroundings. From one of the little bridges he looks down at the water stifled by the spread of a huge flat-leaved yellow lily; it looks almost mutant, he thinks, with fat bright flowers held up on stems as thick as his arm. A young gull flounders unnaturally in the water, as if wounded, but the moorhens and the coots seem to power through the vegetation unconcerned.

Coming down off the bridge he notices the drop in temperature, and wonders if the silence is using the channels as well; probably flowing quicker than choked-up water, he thinks. And the thrashing gull with its open beak looks as if it might well be screaming in pain.

54.

She got off the bus at the wrong stop, and now as she reaches the place she is hot and her canvas bag is much heavier than it had been an hour earlier, and it is getting dark. It takes almost all her courage to get through the front door with the silver key; now she stands in the stairwell, unsure. There are several switches on the wall but she doesn't want to make a mistake, doesn't want to draw attention to herself, and so she climbs the dark stairs very slowly, stopping to breathe and to feel her heart beating too fast, much too fast. Up on the landing she prays no one will come out of the flat opposite and challenge her. I am a friend, she says, over and over in her head, I am a friend of Myra, of Miss Jones; she asked me to keep an eye on the flat for a few days. But she has long since lost any sense of her own right to anything at all, and knows she would not sound convincing. She is so anxious that she has to try the bronze key several times before the lock clicks cleanly and the door opens. She closes it behind her, slips off her shoes with their cracked soles, puts down her bag and finds the light. She likes the place at once.

The little tree is dead, of course, but she waters it anyway and puts it back on the windowsill. Looking down into the darkening street she sees plenty of people, all sorts of people, passing up and down and feels glad; the lights are on in a chip-shop and a foodstore and a pub. She boils the kettle and rummages in her bag for mint tea. Then she pulls off her headscarf and sits on the sofa brushing her grey-black hair, and wondering if she should try and work out how to turn the television on, to get some news of the war. Decides against it, and wanders round the room instead looking at Myra's pictures and books. She likes the photo of her as a little girl, with her mother, probably, sitting on the white steps of a big building, both smiling.

In Myra's bedroom Lina changes into pyjamas and hunts in her bag for the photo of Ali and the kids. Puts it by the bed, and prays, and then curls up to cry, and sleeps, and is surprised to be woken, many hours later, by sunlight on the white sheets.

Today she is not working. Today she will spend her time entirely as she likes. She will wash her clothes, explore the shops in the street below, buy food, fresh fruit and vegetables, and spend hours preparing a meal. She will try out the oven, make an almond cake, with lots of lemon, to take to Myra tomorrow morning. She opens windows all over the flat to let the sunshine in, and hunts around for the cleaning things. It will be so bright in here when Myra comes home, she thinks. It will be so bright. She washes up her cup and watches people down in the street, a young Asian mother and her beautiful son, a builder, two old people not talking to each other. Then a black guy in a dirty anorak ambles past, head to one side, big smile, singing or talking, she can't tell from here; he has two heavy plastic bags, bursting with papers, one in each hand.

55.

An unexpected side effect of the heat wave has been a spike in bench-usage, right across the board. With the Parade behind them, and further action, or so he understands, temporarily suspended, Luke has returned to his former project with considerable enthusiasm. He has just devised a complex system of routes taking in about twenty-five benches, routes which ensure he walks at least 7km a day. He has one of those clever watches which makes sure he covers the distance, and he enters his times in a spreadsheet afterwards – the times vary depending on the people he sees, of course, but it gives you an idea. And, even after three days, he tells Dan, he does feel much fitter, much more focused, and Dan, who spends most of his days pounding the streets with the buggy or traipsing after Teddy in the park, congratulates him.

The spike in usage, though, explains Luke, is definitely temperature-related, so the constituency is not quite the same, more fluid, perhaps less meaningful: they use the benches like pools, dipping in for a few minutes to cool off, they don't stay long, especially if they come in groups or pairs, because of not being able to talk through the silence. And we've finally attached the special thermometers, the ones they ordered last month, to the designated Key Benches, so we can start monitoring the temperatures properly now: most are down to around 5-7 degrees, did you know? And we might even get the viscosity device sorted, if they ever sort out the communications problem with Physics.

They're standing outside the town library, and Luke has been talking non-stop for ten minutes when Teddy wakes and starts to fuss. Dan makes a helpless gesture with his hands, and Luke looks concerned.

I, ah, we don't need to stand here, I could get you a coffee? You could see some of the stats on the iPad.

But Dan just stands there, on the brink of anger, furious with Teddy for waking up, and with Luke, whom he has not seen in days, for wrecking his carefully planned hour. He is also, though he will not admit it, hungry, and tired from not sleeping. His voice is tight.

I'm sorry, he says, I've got three days before we're evicted, and I haven't found a place that'll take us yet. I need to check my emails and try and find some more numbers to ring. And now – he pulls the pram to and fro with slightly too much force, which only makes the child yell louder – and now he's woken up. They're going to love us in there, aren't they?

He turns and pushes the buggy into the library foyer; Teddy is writhing in his straps. Luke is aghast, and runs after them, reaches out for the handle.

Man, you should have told me … about the house … I thought it would have been sorted by now.

I did tell you, a fortnight ago. Nothing's changed.

Teddy's yells get louder. To his great surprise, Luke finds that he has taken control of the buggy and is heading back out to the street.

Come on, he says to Dan, over his shoulder. Come on. We're going to check your emails on my iPad and get some food and, ah, sort you both out.

Dan stands there, breathing hard, and watches them disappear down towards the arcades. Luke doesn't look back again; he has no choice but to run after them. Luke grins as he catches up. Handles like a dream, he says, above the yelling.

Have you seen Lina on your rounds at all? asks Dan.

56.

She is in a big blue sky, looking down on a dark blue sea, and she is spinning so fast it is as if she is not moving at all. She smiles beautifully, confident of keeping it all together; her constituent parts, a hundred, possibly a thousand spinning spheres have coalesced to create her lovely form. If even the smallest one of the spheres, she thinks, were to spin off course, were to be tugged into deep space by a body with a heavier gravitational pull, with an orbit more forceful than the willpower holding her together, then she would disintegrate and the spheres would scatter and travel alone for perhaps centuries before another force in a different part of space pulled a new set of spheres together to make a new form. But she is in equilibrium, she is perfectly balanced, and there will be no question of collapse.

Awake, when she is not practising walking, she knits furiously. The scarf is now absurdly long, but this is the last ball of silky silver wool, so it will have to stop soon. She has lost all inclination to read, and Theo's books stay stacked on the bedside table. His absence defeats her. Ten, eleven days in, it has become uninterpretable, and all she can do is retract like a creature in a shell, for protection. She is very good at not thinking about things, she has had a lot of practice, and it is not hard to divert her thoughts back to the building, which she revisits incessantly, its steps and columns bright in the summer sun. When she can walk again, she thinks, she will sit on those steps in that sun and eat fruit salad. It won't be long now.

And Lina is safe in her flat, and the flat, she thinks, must be glad to have her there. The little tree was dead, of course, but the fridge, she said, wasn't bad at all, and she has opened the windows and let the air in and cleaned the kitchen and the bathroom. You shouldn't be cleaning, said Myra, not after cleaning the way you do all day. This is different, said Lina, this is so very different you have no idea. And they had both cried, and laughed at each other for doing so. This week, though, Lina is doing another ward, so she doesn't see her as much. There is a nice Polish girl with a wide smile who comes most mornings instead.

The huge gull watches her through the window as the nurses come and go, bring tea, bring medicine, bring the dull food, take her blood pressure. The walking must be

tiring her out because she sleeps and sleeps. On three separate occasions this week the duty nurse has come into her
room with a phone in her hand, and found her so deeply
asleep it would, she tells the voice on the other end, be
wrong to wake her. And yes, she says, she'll say who
phoned, don't worry; we'll make sure she gets the message.

57.

He puts the tea down carefully and stands with his hand
on her thin shoulder, looking at what she's done. Huge
sheets of paper cover the table. The lines she draws across
them dance and curve, a dozen or so sketches on every
page; some are discrete and clear – faces, birds – but others
cluster into scenes, small landscapes with foreign-looking
buildings, groups of figures in conversation. Others are
more abstract, or perhaps just unintelligible. Beautiful,
Mam, he says, these are really lovely. She smiles and
reaches up to touch his hand as he squeezes her shoulder
gently. He wonders where they come from, whether she
carries the shapes in her head all the time, or whether they
only happen at the point of contact. He didn't get that gene.

He pulls out one of the finished sheets from the back of
the table and holds it up to the window. Round the edges
are mostly faces and long-legged birds – she was quite well-
known for her birds, at one time – but in the centre, evoked
in a very few lines, is the shape of a woman, naked and
lying on her side. She is staring straight ahead; an indistinct
figure hangs over her, it is not clear who or why. He recognises her, and goes hunting through other pages and finds
her again, twice, lying much in the same position but seen

from slightly different angles. He would like to see her face closer, he thinks; he wonders if she will draw her again.

Who's this, Mam? he asks, without much expectation of a reply. She looks briefly at the picture, and then goes back to her page.

Galatea, she says. Poor girl.

He goes into the hall and phones the hospital one more time. This time it rings and rings and nobody answers at all.

Have you had enough drawing, Mam? he asks after a while. Shall we try and walk a bit in the garden? Be good for your leg, and we could do with some fresh air.

It shouldn't be too hot now, he thinks, late afternoon, the sun has relented. She acquiesces smiling, as she does to almost everything now, it is as if all volition, of body and mind – to eat, to drink, to stand or sleep – must come from him, and everything he suggests she performs willingly, gratefully, as if pleased to have delegated all decision-making to someone else. She forgets to stop, he thinks, she would go on making lines on the paper until she fainted or wet herself. How could he possibly leave her for more than an hour at a time? No one else, no stranger come in to mind her, would be able to know the way he knows what she might need next. Ten, eleven days in, with a routine in place and some of the fear gone, he feels more confident that they could manage this together, day by day; but only if he pulls in his horizons to fit hers, if the house and the pond, the marsh and the woodland are the extent and limits of their shared world. He wouldn't have minded, three or four months back; when most of the few people he has any time for came to him, and the prospect of endlessly shuttling in and out of the city filled him with irritation. The group is experienced enough now for him not to have to do all the pond drops; they're managing OK, he thinks, and from home he can at least deal with the orders, plan the locations, and do what he likes best: the preparation of the tanks, the planting and thinning, the management of the land. Retreat.

But it feels worse than that.

The woman holding onto his arm is as light and thin-boned as a bird. Walking requires the full concentration of both. He guides her to the roses, passionate red. Smell these, Mam, he says, can you smell them?

58.

They pound down the river-path for the third time that day, stopping briefly to admire the heron standing on a stony patch near the weir. *Dak-dak*, says Teddy. Big one, says Dan. Teddy is riding shot-gun on a footplate at the back of the buggy, which holds two black bin-bags full of clothes and saucepans, stuffed toys, plates and mugs and bundles of cutlery wrapped in tea-towels and clothes. The last run.

Mercifully, it rained in the night. The air is breathable again and the entire city feels less irritable. Luke had insisted on getting them a taxi for the main load of boxes, the books, the ancient cd player, the still-unopened box of Jane's things, the dismantled highchair, but Dan was stubborn about doing the rest himself. Three journeys down the path along the river and through the park, past the white buildings of Cathays and through to Luke's new, larger, emptier office where all this stuff can be stashed. Temporarily. Till they find a place. Luke has sent a request round on the University staff list, in case anyone has rooms they're not using. For now, they can have the sofa in his tiny flat. It's a plan. Dan knows that two or three nights with a hyped-up restless toddler in the living room will be enough; Teddy does not go to sleep willingly.

Near the castle they stop for the third time to say hello to the JCB and Rhod, who finds their unconventional method of moving house amusing. What are you doing all this for? asks Dan.

Keeping the water under control, he says. They want it away from the walls; they think it's damaging the foundations.

Dan looks at the ugly, emptied moat. And is it?

Course not. It's a daft idea. And there's plenty else happening round here; haven't you seen they're mending the railings, right round the park?

Dan thinks of his gap into the dark starry fields closing up. They say goodbye to Rhod and leave the park; pushing hard and fast through the wall of cold on the way out. As they pass the museum Teddy hops off the back and runs along the lower steps. His chatter does not stop; the thick channel of silence must still be up nearer the top.

Most of their stuff can be pushed under the desks and tables hard up against the walls round the edge, but the office, nevertheless, looks quite a bit smaller and less empty. Black bin bags are never a good look, he thinks. More cardboard boxes would have been less conspicuous. Luke comes in balancing two cups of coffee and a beaker of milk and some digestives and tries not to look too alarmed. It won't be long, says Dan. I promise.

While they are talking and Dan is offering to cook supper there's a quick knock and the door opens. The professor looks surprised. I'll come back later, he says, withdrawing. Apologies.

No, no, says Luke, going slightly red, I'm not, ah, busy. Shall I come and find you in your office? Five minutes? The professor nods and looks with courteous curiosity at Dan and Teddy, who seem familiar.

Ah, this is Dan, says Luke, and ah, Teddy. They're in the middle of moving house, and this is just temporary, I thought it would be OK, in the office here, you know...

He nods again. I think we must have met, he says, and smiles.

Dan says nothing, but smiles back and shrugs. He lifts Teddy up onto the desk beside him and holds him tight round the middle.

Dan's been helping out with the, ah, benches project? says Luke, making it sound like a question. He collected a lot of stats for me a while back, and he's been keeping an eye, you know?

It's BenchMarks I want to talk to you about, says the professor. There is something in his tone.

Not Lina, thinks Dan, in a sudden rush of fear. Please, not Lina. He bundles Teddy into his arms and stands up.

We'll go and get the stuff for the curry, he says. See you later. He nods at the professor, and leaves them to it.

59.

The silence has claimed its first fatality. The red-haired boy, too drunk or wasted to feel the cold, had gone to sleep on a bench too close to the castle, with his head pillowed on his rucksack, and had not woken up. Perverse, really, to die of hypothermia in August. It had taken quite a long time for anyone in the flow of people hurrying past to realise; someone with a medical background, apparently, had eventually noticed the colour of his face and done something about it.

But there is nothing he can do about it. Worse, the things that were being done, the connections made, the useful partnerships with the science departments, the energetic efforts of his own team, all seem to be failing or thwarted or breaking down. When he had finally cornered the reluctant VC she had said it was out of her power now, that they had been obliged to back off, and that backing off was the right thing to do. And when he pushed her, gently, insistently, she had sudden tears in her eyes. The park, she said, the playing fields; they made it quite clear they could revoke the agreement, or push up the price we pay on the student swipe-cards, and then there are the leases in Cathays...You know as well as I do they could bring us to our knees in months. I said you would back off, what else was there to say? And there's an injunction of some sort on your maps. God knows. You have to leave the castle alone, they said; the silence isn't their doing, they've got their own people working on it, and they don't want that kind of publicity. She shook her head abruptly as if trying to shake something out of it, and held her hands up in front of her face for protection.

So he is looking out of the window of a train at five in the morning, heading for breakfast with Meg in Crewe. Beyond that, a long way beyond, the Highlands, and a weekend at the Lodge, courtesy of the old lady, he isn't even quite sure which one, who had taken a violent fancy to him at some public event or other. More power, apparently, in her crooked little finger, than all the phoney Boards and Trusts put together. Desperate measures, he thinks, god, these are desperate remedies. Poor kid. Though it would doubtless have happened anyway, as Luke said, he never looked terribly likely to be a survivor. He scrolls down his phone to find Meg's last message. She will come as far as Crewe, she says, and no further, no time, with the kids still off school and the troupe rehearsing furiously for September. He has a glimpse of her in the huge vaulted granary, the ropes and lights like a crazed web from floor to ceiling, as ruthless as Rodin with her performers, twisting their beautiful bodies in the air. And grins to think of her, an unlikely trainspotter, implausibly quick to find him the times and itinerary all the way to Fort William: do it now, she says, or it will be too late. Who would have thought it, in this day and age, that you could still get all that way, that there would still be trains. He stretches the vertebrae in his tired back like a cat and watches the pale grey morning wash the trees and fields with a delicate light, and wonders when it might be possible to get a coffee, however unpalatable, and wonders if he has the necessary strength of mind to get what he needs from the weekend ahead.

She looks five years younger than the last time they met. Seven. Perhaps the light is better here than in St Pancras, he thinks; but he knows with a pang of envy that it is the month in the mountains, curative, restorative, home. Not his, for such a long time now. He does not like to be reminded of what he is missing.

Look how tired you are, she says with her hands, accusingly.

Entirely your fault, making me get up at four.

Oh but it'll be wonderful, the train beyond Glasgow, you'll see. Worth it.

And then. He shudders. What then?

Be cool. Do as they do. Tell them what you want in pieces, unravel it gently. And do the same with what you have to offer; give it to them bit by bit.

She hands over the file, and pulls a face. Here, she says with her eyes; and then taps the rest onto the screen. The tailored version: a performance for the castle, site-specific, one-off, a private viewing, at my lady's pleasure. See if she bites.

Oh, I expect she bites, he says grimly. He takes the file and flicks through the first few pages, then looks up at her and smiles. Hey, he says. Hey. *Diolch.*

60.

And now, the corridor. It stretches from the door of her room into impossible distance. But there are waymarkers, targets to aim for; a few strategic posters, doors off to other rooms, and a little way down, the entrance to the lift. Cruelly, no chairs. She must not overdo it, she thinks. She is perfectly aware of the lure of walking in straight lines.

To help keep her balance, she focuses her mind on walking another line, the long polished stone wall marking the edges of the museum, low and broad and easy for a child to run along, the pale building rising on one side, her mother keeping pace on the other. Even harder, no doubt, for a brittle young woman in high heels. She hasn't tried it recently. But she remembers leaves dropping around her, back when she was the living twin of the pensive little girl in bronze. Falling leaves would unbalance anybody, she thinks. All those directions, none of them yours.

Exactly as predicted, and distracted by the falling leaves, she lets the polished stone wall take her much too far. She stops defeated just short of the lift, waiting for her legs to crumple and leave her ignominiously on the floor of the corridor until a rare nurse, or a rarer visitor, comes along and helps her to her feet. But then the lift lights up and thrums into life, travelling upwards, clunking to a halt. The door slides open and the first thing out is the cleaning trolley, and the second thing out is Lina, who is alarmed, and then delighted.

Well look, she says, look at you!

Too far, says Myra dimly, glued to the wall.

Come on, says Lina, gently supporting her thin waist and guiding her to the trolley; help me push this thing back to your room, it's not so far, and look, I've made you a cake.

Once Myra is sat up against her pillows, and Lina is busy cleaning round her, they catch up. The guy in the shop opposite, says Lina, keeps giving me free fruit; look, two more lemons. I think he likes me. Myra laughs out loud through a mouthful of cake, not him! she says, it can't be the same guy – he's a grumpy sod.

Not with me, says Lina primly, picking up a letter in order to clean the surface of the bedside table. You haven't opened this, look. When did you get it?

It's her work address. Myra looks puzzled, then frowns. I thought that was a dream, she says. Since people stopped coming to see me I tend to dream them instead. She must have been real that time. Work colleague. The difficult one.

She reaches for the envelope and looks at it dispassionately. Oh, I remember this now, I know what it says; we're supposed to apply for our own jobs, except there are fewer of them. Like musical chairs.

And will you?

She shrugs. I have no idea, she says. I can't imagine much outside this room.

Well the corridor's a start, says Lina, turning to go. You'll have to take it from there, bit by bit. I have to go now, but I'll try and find someone to get you a cup of tea. She doesn't sound particularly hopeful.

Lovely cake, says Myra, thank you.

Your oven took some getting used to, says Lina, the first one was a mess. Get some sleep now; you'll be worn out, all that exercise.

But Myra has thought of something, and is sliding out of bed trying to find her handbag. Lina goes back over. What is it now, she says, here, let me help. The phone, says Myra, fishing it out and putting it in Lina's hand; it is cold and heavy, old-fashioned, quite dead. There must be a charger in the flat somewhere, she says, in a drawer in the kitchen. Or still plugged in by the bed. Can you find it?

Wake this thing up? We could swap numbers, at least, you and me.

Lina looks at the phone in her hand, and shakes her head. Mine's gone, she says. I can't find it anywhere. I think the girls in the hostel took it. It was no good anyway. No one from my family had that number in the first place, so they would never have found me, even if there is anyone left to find me. She looks across at Myra and smiles. But you should start talking to people. Lots of people. I'll find that charger.

If he were ever to come back, thinks Myra, settling back into the pillows and closing her eyes, then I would make quite certain he knows how to find me again.

61.

They travel through space together. The universe rushes past them on either side. Teddy wriggles in his father's lap, and waves his hands as if conducting: stars coming, he calls out, stars coming stars coming stars coming. They stay just long enough for the earth to take shape and form in the void, and then leave the rest of the audience, two patient Japanese girls and an elderly German, to find out what happens next. They know what happens next, and it is not half so interesting, not to them. Nappy change, then coffee in the main hall so Teddy can climb the sweeping white stairs, up and down, up and down. It is nice, thinks Dan, that he still hasn't discovered the shop. At the top of the main flight of stairs the bronze statue of Labour, a pretty young man leaning wearily on his hoe, looks into middle distance and does not pay them much regard.

Dan wonders, with subtle regret, why Teddy doesn't seem to need a nap after lunch these days, even after toddler group this morning, their first time back in about three or four weeks, the pair of them, inevitably, much fussed over. But the move has changed so much, their old routines are gone. And there is not much point, he thinks, in trying to settle him into new ones, since they'll have to be moving again soon. If he can find somewhere. Though Luke insists he doesn't mind. Their evenings are enjoyable, the child curled up asleep in a duvet-nest in the corner and them talking over beers, swapping music, films, and Luke reading out good bits from books he likes, until Dan thinks that it might, one day, be possible to read for pleasure again. The slow Californian drawl reciting sections from that crazy man Fort, stars and planets and impossible conglomerations of objects, showers of frogs and little fish raining periodically from the sky. Spinning worlds up there in space and Fort's own life by then so tightly circumscribed you can count the steps: home, library, home. To boxes and boxes of cuttings and clippings where all the anomalies are stashed. Poor man, he thinks, he would have loved databases as much as Luke does. Retrievable knowledge.

The coffee today is another pleasure. He is beginning to relax, the anxieties retracting their sharp little claws from his heart. Only the thought of Lina really nags at him now; they had gone straight to the Blaschkas this morning, even before Jane's stars, and walked around them several times, as if performing a spell. She hadn't materialised. Have you seen a woman in a headscarf, he had wanted to ask the attendant, as if women in headscarves were so very rare you would have to notice, but he had not had the courage. She is never on her bench, and the number he had for her rings meaninglessly: texts fly off into nowhere, bringing nothing back. If she has moved on, he thinks, we will never know. And if it is worse than that. Luke told him about the ginger-haired boy, and he is intermittently wounded by the thought of those blank eyes. I should have tried to talk to him, he thinks. But I was frightened.

He drinks the coffee slowly, and watches Teddy on the steps. He isn't looking forward to having to move again, it's all so cumbersome, but he is less angry now at the loss of the little terraced house with the blue door. They'll find somewhere. And he's nearly ready again to think about doing some work for Theo, the digging would be good for him, and the company, and they could do with some proper fresh air, and there'll be new creatures in the pond for Teddy to examine. Theo might have seen her, he thinks, of course. They might be working on something together. He hunts back through his phone for the number and wonders what he should say.

Sorry been out of touch. Do you need a hand digging? Have you seen Lina?

He presses send, and reaches for his mug and looks around him. In the time it has taken him to write the text, Teddy has disappeared.

62.

A woman so careful of everything does not simply lose her phone. Careful of her speech, since the language, though familiar, is not her own; careful of her undemonstrative appearance, of her manners, of the little money she has. She has hunted all around the flat in case the anxiety and excitement of arrival had perhaps made her do something unusual. Her bag, her pockets, are turned out several times over, as if the thing might somehow have materialised from one search to the next. She picks up the useless charger from where it sits coiled neatly by the photo of Ali and the children, and knows that she has not plugged it in since moving. She tries it in Myra's phone, but of course it does not fit. She has a vivid memory of seeing her phone in her handbag the day before she left the hostel. A cheap, worthless phone, no use to anyone else; only spite would make you steal such a phone. But it had a number, the number beneath her staring face on the Middle East Displaced Persons site, a number which made it at least possible to imagine that one day somebody might get in touch. She is daunted by the loss and the complications that will ensue. She needs to talk to someone, to Dan, to get advice in sorting this out.

The train she is on should be helping, she thinks, its rhythms relaxing her, releasing the anxious knot in her stomach. The scenes through the grey-streaked window should be at the very least a distraction, roads and factories, hillsides, horses, rivers, pylons. None of it looks at all familiar, she thinks, though last time, with Teddy in her lap, she had pointed things out. A yellow crane. Some sheep. But there is nothing she recognises here. Perhaps it is the change in the season that makes it look so different. Or perhaps she has misremembered the name of the place, and is heading in the wrong direction altogether, into a hinterland not Theo's world of bogs and streams and moss and forests, but one of warehouses and roundabouts and junkyards and defunct petrol stations. Perhaps there are two different places with the same name. She looks in her bag again, in case the phone has reappeared; she finds a very old boiled sweet, gone sticky in its wrapper, and sucks it slowly.

This morning, though it feels much longer ago than that, she had walked from Myra's flat into town, and then found her way out to the street with the house with the blue door. It was covered in scaffolding. Tenants been gone at least three weeks, love, said the man carrying paint. The lady's doing it up to sell now, see.

She had gone to the museum, forcing herself through the wall of silence, more brutal than ever now she carried her own cold fear twisted inside her. Strange and beautiful plants and animals had distracted her for a while, but she had not found Dan and Teddy. She had sat, then, on her old bench until the cold had beaten her away. And finally she had decided on Theo, catching the train as one might say a prayer: an act of faith, from a platform she recognised, with a ticket to a name that sounded familiar. And when she gets there, she thinks, if there is where she ought to be, she will have to walk and ask people for directions. The house was a long way from the station, she remembers, he had come to get them in his van. She must not close her eyes, now, in case she misses her stop.

And when it comes it is miraculously familiar, recognisable, a place she has definitely been before. She stands in front of the little station in the full heat of the day and looks down the street and up at the hills and wonders what to do next. She should eat something, obviously, but her anxiety is pushing her on, she must keep walking, though she has done too much today already, and the thin flat shoes, not made for walking, have begun to rub her heels. This is where he picked us up, she thinks. I can remember which way he turned out of the station. I will recognise the road, I was in the front, I think I will know which way to turn.

She has the sense to buy a bottle of water and some biscuits from the station cafe, and then she sets off and soon leaves the small town straggling behind. She walks along the edge of the road, pulling in when cars pass, always too quickly. Nobody stops. There are green clustered berries in the hedges, and a feathery, sweet-scented creamy flower growing along the verge; crisp packets and polystyrene cartons are scattered in the long grass. Gates into fields with cows. Patches of woodland, oak trees thick with leaves. Her heels are rubbed raw, but she is too ashamed to take off her shoes and walk barefoot on a public road. After a while there is a junction, with a sign pointing to several named places, which she scans critically for a moment or two, and then ignores, carrying on along the main road. A second junction holds her attention for longer, and after a long minute's thought she takes it, off to the left, a smaller road dipping down into a valley. The road is narrower here, and the cars fewer, and by now her heels are wet with blood and she has no choice but to take off her shoes. She hunkers under a tree and sips some water, eats a biscuit, and hopes she has taken the right turning. The place looks utterly unfamiliar again, a narrow lane between trees which could be going anywhere, and too low down in this wooded valley for the open slopes and views around Theo's pond, but she cannot face trekking back to the main road now. The soles of her feet feel scratched and bruised as well, but when she tries the shoes again the pain of the gouged-out heels is still worse.

Eventually there is a stone bridge over a small river, and a path leading down to the riverbank, where she washes her face and then sits with her feet in cool running water, grateful beyond words. If she is right, she thinks, though she feels less and less sure now that this is the case, then the water round her feet could have come down from his pond. She is comforted by the thought of a million micro-organisms brushing her skin. But all these valleys have rivers, she thinks, even in this heat, even in the driest summer; it is not like it is at home. And when she is rested, she starts a slow, winding climb, and her thoughts are all of her own country, of walking as a child with her mother up a dry rocky path, cutting through terraces of olive groves to visit her grandmother, who was blind and angry and who frightened her; she remembers how they walked to visit her with gifts of fruit through the thick noise of the cicadas, the heavily-scented herbs. So when the road finally shakes off the last of the trees, and suddenly splits to accommodate a huge grey and white chapel surrounded by gravestones, she stands for a brief moment in two simultaneous worlds, rocked by the force of a double recognition. This is not a place you forget, after all. The name carved in stone and picked out in white letters above her is *Hebron*.

63.

He reaches across the water and carefully pulls the reed

stem out with the larval case intact and empty, still gripping for dear life. He slides it gently from the stalk and cradles it in the palm of his big hand, noting the species, another Southern Hawker, perhaps one of the two he'd caught in a flashing blue-and-yellow dogfight at the far end of the pond yesterday morning. He regrets not having been there to see the creature split its skin, but in years of patient watching he has only caught a few such moments of emergence.

He takes the fragile exuvia back over to the hut, labels and dates it and puts it in the appropriate box. Then he continues his slow inspection of the pond edge, noting tiny white moths, the various signs of water vole, spider-webs, tortoiseshell butterflies on the pink flowers of watermint, slugs. A couple of wrens fuss in the thicket of brambles, where the blackberries are just beginning to redden. He tries not to think of Myra, and thinks instead of his mother's drawings; two more recurring images intrigue him, a woman's face made up entirely of spheres, a face you can only see if you stand far enough away; a naked girl with a curious expression trapped by or emerging from a rough block of stone. She is still doing birds, the long-legged birds, but he has long been familiar with them.

A flash of blue scrapes the corner of his eye. He spins round to catch it, misses it, but stands and waits a moment. Patience. They often come back. And this one does, confirming his subconscious thrill, because it is an Emperor, as blue as lapis lazuli, absurdly huge, flying with dipped abdomen, scouring the pond. Oh you perfect beauty, he thinks, as it circles and dances and scoots off to the sedges at the far end, are you just visiting, or do you belong here, are you one of mine?

And it seems to Theo impossible, and quite ridiculous, that there should be no way of telling Myra about this. He has phoned the hospital every single day, and no one will tell him, in a way that convinces him, exactly where or how she is. He turns abruptly and walks back to the wooden house. He takes a sheet from a pile of rough paper and sits down to it, determined. Myra, he writes, *there was an Emperor dragonfly over the pond. You never saw anything so utterly blue in your life. When you're well again I'll show you, and I'll come and find you as soon as I can but it's difficult with my mother. Please ring, I have left messages. Please ring. Theo.* And his number.

He closes and latches the summerhouse and heads quickly up the path. He is pleased to find her still drawing. Mam, he says, turning his piece of paper over to the blank side. Here. Do me a dragonfly. She looks puzzled. He fetches a book down from the corner shelf. Dragonfly, he says. Emperor. *Anax imperator.* Do me one, can you? I'm going to find an envelope.

And when he comes back downstairs she has drawn two, in mid-air, over the barest outline of a pond. He kisses her, delighted, and addresses the envelope. I'm going to the village to get milk and supper and post this, Mam, he says. Fifteen minutes. I won't be long. You sit tight and I'll bring you some Rich Teas and we'll have a cup of something when I get back.

And he is gone in the van before he has even had time to think. She normally comes with him to the village, sitting in the van while he shops, but today he is barely stopping, and he knows she will be happy drawing for another half an hour at least. He can't remember when the post goes, prays god he is not too late. Slowing down to cross the junction at the foot of the hill he half sees a distant figure, off to his left, like a shadow, walking along the edge of the road. But with the letter on his dashboard and a flash of blue in his head he pushes down on the accelerator and thinks nothing of it.

64.

I did what was required.

The west coast slips away from him and he lets it go. He has no business with such beauty, with birds and horizons and rocks of almost shocking three-dimensionality in slanting sea-reflected light. He makes no attempt to hold any of it, refuses to let it imprint. On the way up he had imagined stopping for a few hours at one of these places to explore; a half-formed plan that had sustained him for the first part of the long weekend. By now all he wants is the entire length of the British Isles between himself and the people in the big house. Cardiff may not be far enough. Hills and farmhouses and motorways and dry-stone walls and power stations, fried chicken shops, shopping malls, builders' merchants, wind-turbines – anything, everything will do.

He begins to run, in his head, the longest and most complex route he knows from his office to the flat through the park, but even the park, he thinks, is only there by their grace, by their favour; so he swerves off onto an imaginary road to nowhere, long and straight and heading into some vast American landscape, and keeps on running. *North by Northwest*, he thinks, they'll be sending the plane over any minute now.

The Scottish coast is so insistent he closes his eyes to avoid it, and finds, when they open again, that he has bought himself an hour's oblivion, and is grateful. Every hour, and every mile, he thinks, pushes it all a hair's breadth further away.

I did what was required.

Seven, maybe eight hours ago he had sent her the barest of messages. Three consecutive dates in mid-September. Enough for her to know she has just under a month. She will have started preparations already. Silk and scaffolding. A stage like a pool of light. She will know what train he is on, and be expecting to hear from him, a line of relief, of quiet triumph, of bitter humour. But his phone has been off since midnight, when he had sent the text, dressed himself for the journey and gone to sit and wait for morning and his train in the chair by the window, wrapped in a blanket, phoney tartan, under a pale scattering of stars. He closes her out of his mind to protect her, to protect himself. Keep running, he thinks, and this time it is along the nondescript length of a canal, past grand industrial derelictions of blackened brick, under road-bridges and railway lines. Dandelion and dock, the vegetation of neither here nor there. Another long straight line, this one, no complex labyrinthine route through streets and parks; he imagines his breathing, heavier and rougher in his chest with every half-mile, like breathing sandpaper. Keep running. Another hair's-breadth.

There is a boy on the towpath up ahead, perhaps ten years old, fishing, and he has caught something big enough to be visible from a way off. He slackens the pace, to see what happens next, though it doesn't take him long to realise that he knows what happens next: the twisting fish, open-mouthed, and the frightened child's botched attempt to kill it. A pen-knife. Then a rock. Neither wholly successful. He runs on past himself and does not look back.

65.

Luke arrives, precariously, on a bicycle borrowed from a student. Teddy has been missing for more than half an hour now, and the museum authorities have called the police. A picture from Dan's phone has been sent out to all staff, and in every gallery attendants are looking for a little boy in blue dungarees with silky blond hair. Dan has searched all the rooms, climbed all the stairs, public and not public, right up to the dizzy octagonal balcony where the directors' offices and the panelled meeting rooms are; he has looked dispassionately at the cinematic drop to the tiled floor below, pushed at the door of the Galatea Room, still closed, and hurried on, trying to outstrip the slow cold disbelief spreading through his nervous system like poison.

He is so terribly easy to imagine in so many different

settings. Teddy trotting oblivious under a row of bright Impressionists; watched over by concerned Madonnas, crouched hide-and-seeking under a bench. Teddy talking to the stuffed foxes, the seabirds; Teddy listening to the mellifluous tones of the Turtle. Reaching up to touch shining minerals, stroking a mammoth leg-bone. Asleep in the buggy by the table where they had coffee. Teddy sitting on the floor waiting patiently by his mother's stars. Dan passes a toilet and goes in to retch up his fear. He can feel himself shutting down. He splashes water on his face, and finds his way mechanically down to the main hall, where a policewoman is waiting to talk to him, and where Luke finally finds him and holds him in a bear hug, hard.

They sit him down with a glass of water and the policewoman begins asking him questions, slowly, patiently, and purely, he thinks, to keep him there. He is too tired to fight or make a scene now, and so he sits and answers her as best he can, all the while watching from a distance, from up near the dome of the ceiling, watching himself and the policewoman doing everything properly. Very slowly. And then he sees Luke quietly head off to the desk to exchange a word with two or three tight-faced staff as they hold their phones and their walkie-talkies and wait for news.

Luke is asking about the outside of the building. The exits are blocked, they say, and the police are searching the area, though it does seem unlikely that such a small boy would have wandered out by himself. And would he have got through the silence? It's pretty thick still, especially at the front there; you'd think it might deter him. They look at the picture on their phones, and hope that it isn't going to become the iconic vanished child picture in tomorrow's news.

I'll go, ah, and see if I can help outside, he says. Just for ten minutes. He glances across at Dan. Tell him ...Tell him I'll be right back. Can, ah, someone let me out here? They give him a neck tag, and open the door.

He's wearing a T-shirt, and is still hot and sweating from cycling, so the cold of the silence is a shock. He catches his breath and pushes through it to stand just the other side. Two policemen on the lower steps are turning people away from the main entrance. Then he sits down and pulls up the most recent map of the silence on his iPad, homing in on the thick loop around the building. He experiments with different ways of zooming in, magnifying the line of emptiness to try and capture its edges, which are slightly fuzzy, slightly ragged, perhaps because the stuff is in flux, he thinks. He steps back into it, and the screen goes blank. Then he steps out again and, holding the iPad like a map, starts to walk along the edge, a bit like following a river, he thinks, but with the river as high as a wall and invisible – higher than head height, nobody can quite work out how high. What am I looking for anyway, he thinks; why would Teddy be here?

It isn't easy to follow the silence exactly round the building, as various architectural features get in the way, especially at the front; but it gets easier walking up Museum Avenue along the low stone wall, easier to move in and out, to trace the line precisely. It seems, as at the front, to keep about a foot away from the building itself, but there are places where it brushes up against the stone, and others where the coldness collects and pools, swirling back on itself. The staff entrance, down the slope at the back, is like a small dark lake. He spends five minutes there, though plenty of other people are looking in the corners and behind the parked cars, and shivers as he climbs the steps up the side, following the silence as it snakes back up, cutting off the building from the visitors' car park, and coiling round towards the bulge of the lecture theatre on Park Place. He follows another low wall, and turns at last onto the front steps, where he waves his badge at the police, and is about to push through the doors when he sees, just ahead of him, shuffling slowly across the Gorsedd gardens, a familiar bundled figure clutching two grubby plastic bags bursting with papers. He hesitates for a second, wonders about going to talk to him; but he is coming from the wrong direction, he thinks. He can't possibly have seen Teddy.

66.

The long walk down the corridor left her worn out; she has spent the last two days more or less in bed. Small flurries of doctors and nurses, more than has been usual lately, have been taking blood and measuring things. And there was a trip to some other part of the hospital to be scanned again. All of which, they seemed to agree, counts as progress. No Lina, which she regrets though half expected. She knows her hours have been cut. But the Polish girl with the wide smile is back, and on the second day, watching her empty the tangled red hair from the bin, Myra asks her what her name is, and how long she has been in Cardiff.

Two years, says Dorota. Yes. Nearly two years.

Have you been cleaning all this time?

She shakes her head and smiles. No, I work in a hairdressers, up near the castle. Closed down now. I am training there. Back home, near Gdansk, I will open a *salon*. She says it the French way, and gives a little wave of her long fingers, and it all sounds utterly plausible.

Myra nods approval. That sounds good, she says. I'm sorry your old place closed down. You looking for another salon to work in?

Looking, she says with a shrug. But a lot is closing down out there. Maybe I'll go home sooner.

Myra touches her own hair. This is no good, she says. You see how it's coming out. Do you think…?

Dorota comes over and gently feels a strand of Myra's hair.

Beautiful hair, she says. But yes. If we cut it short short it will come back one day stronger.

Myra nods, says nothing.

I come back this evening after work, says Dorota. With my scissors.

The trolley trundles off down the corridor towards the lift, and Myra curls back under the sheets, suddenly sad for her poor hair. She feels her mother insistently brushing out the tangles before school, yelling at her to just be still.

Sleep this time takes her directly to her bench, where she sits swinging her legs and feeling hot and thirsty, watching her mother and a man walk round and round the big stones, talking. There are bright flowers in the beds and people coming and going. After a while she gets up and stands in front of the little bronze girl, who is crouched on her plinth with her arms wrapped round her legs, and her chin resting on her knees, thinking hard. She stands there for a long time, a minute, maybe two. Then she touches the girl's hand very lightly, and gets back on her bench, sitting sideways this time, so she can pull her own knees up and put her chin down, and wait for her mother to finish talking.

But she doesn't finish talking, she goes on and on, round and round the stones, deep in discussion, not looking up or over at the bench, where the little girl finally lets go of her grazed knees and lies down to sleep.

67.

The letter slips into the box in time. He wishes it luck and speed. Then he goes back to queue up in the village shop, holding milk and biscuits and a packet of frozen peas, feeling disproportionately large, and listening to the chatter around him, dipping and drifting between English and Welsh. He moves forward a few paces, and the phone in his jacket pocket collects a sudden burst of messages as it finds a little pool of connectivity. He balances groceries in one huge hand, and scans through as best he can with the other. Dan's text from earlier that afternoon is among them. It would be a blessing, he thinks, to see them both. Back at the van he quickly answers those who need it, and then writes to Dan to tell him they can come out any time; and no, he hasn't seen Lina.

He is calm enough now to drive home leisurely, with a detour down the valley to collect two more gas canisters and some fuel for the strimmer. The path around the pond needs clearing again, especially if Teddy is imminent. He follows a pair of jays back up the tiny lane to the house. More blue flashes. As he loops around the big mulberry tree to park on the dandelion and gravel drive he sees in surprise, then in fear, that the front door is standing wide open, like a dark astonished mouth. She has escaped, he thinks. Wandered out to find me. But surely not far, and not down the road... The garden. Probably the garden. She can't have made it to the pond. If she has fallen. Her leg. I should have bloody locked her in.

He slams the van door shut and looks around for guidance. In the time it takes him to begin to think, two figures appear in the doorway. They smile at him. Lina looks smaller than he remembers, and oddly ragged, and tearstained; his mother, taller by a head, rests a protective arm around her shoulders. He leaps up the steps towards them and hugs them both together. What happened? he said. Where did you come from? Are you OK? Lina, what happened?

I'll make some tea, says his mother unexpectedly. Then turns and points:

Her feet.

Theo sees the blood on Lina's heels and the ruined little shoes by the door. He guides her gently inside towards the sofa, and sits her down.

No rush now, he says. Let's have a look at this.

He goes out to the kitchen to fetch a bowl of warm water and finds his mother stood looking at the tea-pot and the kettle. He spoons some loose tea into the pot and fills it, and points at the cupboard. Can you get us three cups, Mam? He holds up three fingers. That would be great. Then he finds a clean towel, lint and bandages from upstairs, and begins to tend Lina's wounded feet. The sight of such a large, awkward man kneeling in front of her makes her sob.

It's OK, he says, come on now, you'll be fine. We'll have some tea and you can tell me what's going on. You must have walked miles.

I didn't know she was your mother, says Lina through her tears.

Well she's not as ugly as me, says Theo cheerfully, not looking up. But yes, we're related.

Now she laughs and cries all at once. No, she says, I mean when she was in hospital. I didn't know she was your mother. Mrs Evans.

He leaves off bandaging her foot and looks up at her in puzzlement.

What do you mean?

In the hospital. Where I clean. Mrs Evans was on my round.

She smiles.

We had good conversations. I was sorry when she went, but I'm glad her leg is better.

Various things dawn on him simultaneously, and he gets to his feet in agitation.

At the hospital? Where my mother...? Cleaner? Lina, I didn't know. Of course of course ... she let you in. Oh, Lina...

He crouches back down again and grabs both of her hands in his; his incoherence deepens.

I ... do you know a girl with red hair, very pale? She's on the cancer ward ... is that part of your ... I mean, have you seen her, is she...?

Lina pulls her hands free so she can put them firmly on his big shoulders. I know Myra, she says. Of course I know Myra.

The shock of her name.

I...

She's getting better, I'm sure she is. She's making herself walk. To get out. It won't be long.

By now he is next to her on the sofa with his head in his hands. Two weeks, he says. Two weeks, I ring every bloody day but no one answers. And I can't go into town because I can't leave... He gestures helplessly. Why doesn't she phone me here?

Tea, says his mother brightly across the room. Theo helps Lina to her feet, and she limps over to the table.

Thank you, Mrs Evans.

The older women smiles at her, and then at her son. Do you take milk? she asks him.

He closes his eyes. No, Mam. Not now, not ever.

No phone, says Lina, answering Theo's question. She can't phone, it's run out, dead. And the nurses, they hardly ever come now. It's hard even to get her a cup of tea.

I need to see her.

I know. I can stay here. We'll be fine.

He is looking at the clock and calculating time and distance.

It's late. It will be late.

He looks at Lina, still dishevelled and tear-stained. Her clothes are covered in dust. At his mother, smiling intently at something or somebody just beyond them both. He takes a deep breath.

Tomorrow, he says. Come on, you need to eat and rest; and I'll show you the house and get you settled in. I'll go first thing tomorrow. Mam will be happy with you here.

Relief lifts him like a wave. And while Lina is washing and changing into some of his mother's old clothes he puts fish in the oven and peels potatoes. Remembers Dan. Fetches his jacket and slips out the back door, climbing the hill behind the house as fast as he can to the spot where the phone usually works.

Lina is here, he writes. She's fine. Come and join us.

The sky west behind the rowan-tree hill the other side

171

of the valley is streaked with red. Fort's rivers of blood, he thinks, *that vein albuminous seas.* The arteries of Gene-sistrine: *sunsets are consciousness of them... super-embryonic reservoirs from which life-forms emanate...*

At this moment, anything is possible. I'll show you soon, he tells Myra in his head. Soon.

As he sets off down the hill another late message comes through. From Dan. Inscrutably brief, and frightening: *Teddy is lost,* it says.

68.

The building emptied out its public an hour early, and most of the staff, those not part of the volunteer search group, have gone by now as well. The police and the volunteers have been methodically working their way through room after room. Dan is still at a table in the main hall. He has stopped talking or reacting altogether, but when Luke suggests they walk once round the Gorsedd gardens he lets himself be pulled gently through the main door and down the steps. In the park they find the black guy on Myra's bench, being interrogated by two frustrated policemen. Luke intervenes.

Ah, excuse me? We know this man, he's part of a university project; can we, ah, help you?

He's not co-operating, says the first policeman. He won't tell us how long he's been here, so we can't rule him out.

And, says the second policeman, he won't stop singing.

Luke checks his watch. Ah, about two hours and twenty minutes, he says. I saw him arrive earlier. About an hour after the kid went missing. I don't think he will know anything.

Who is he? says the second policeman. He won't tell us his name.

This is Mr Jones, says Luke. Nehemiah Jones.

Dan adds, quietly, but you can call him Skip. He nods at the figure on the bench, who grins and winks at him, and gestures that he should come and sit down. *Hallelujah*, he says. Dan shakes his head. The policemen look slightly uncomfortable, make professional-sounding noises, and withdraw. Dan sits down in his misery beside Skip, who shifts one of his dirty bags along to make room. Luke shows him a picture of Teddy. We've lost him, Mr Jones, he says. He's gone.

He watches the man's face slowly cloud over; he rustles through one of the plastic bags and after a while pulls out a picture of the professor from about five years ago, newly appointed as Director of the School of Cultural Cartography, looking shiny and determined.

Jesus, he says, is a mighty good saviour.

That's not Jesus, says Luke.

And anyway, says Dan, bitter and already shivering, he isn't; he's patently useless. Don't give us the Jesus stuff now, for christ's sake.

Skip's eyes are filling up with tears, and after putting his picture away he starts to sing again, hoarse and low, a jumble of desolate bits and pieces about hard times and the killing floor and the people who are drifting from door to door. He rocks back and forth.

When the policewoman comes out to check up on Dan she finds him sitting with his eyes closed, pale and completely still, with the man on the bench beside him rocking and keening. *In the pines*, he sings, *in the pines.* Luke is on another bench a few yards away, comparing maps on his iPad. He looks up at her and smiles.

Hi, he says. He's OK here; best if you leave him be. And I've just thought of something. I need to go back inside. Would you, ah, just keep an eye? Don't sit too long, though, or you'll get cold.

She sits down neatly on the bench and folds her hands over her walkie-talkie as if it were a prayer book.

Where the sun never shines.

And shiver the whole night through.

She shivers.

Ten minutes later her walkie-talkie crackles. She can hear nothing through the interference, so she moves away from the bench, turning towards the building. At that moment Luke appears on the top step, with Teddy limp in his arms, asleep or unconscious. He is yelling for Dan, though no sound reaches them at all through the silence. She cries out and drops the walkie-talkie and runs over to the bench, pulling Dan roughly out of his cold trance.

Come on, she says. Quick now. They've found him.

69.

He lies under a sheet, too cold and then too hot, letting the poison of the weekend work its way through him as illness. He cannot read. Music is unbearable, and the voices on the radio cannot be endured for more than two minutes. He shrinks like a coward from the news. When he phoned the office he had warned them that it might take three days. This is already the third; at least he thinks it is the third. He sleeps as much as possible, and eats almost nothing, and wonders how long it will all go on. He can feel her restlessness, trapped inside his phone, his iPad, his laptop, volleys of questions and comments swirling around like starlings, light and teasing at first, then increasingly disturbed. But he has built a glass wall around her, to keep her safe, to keep her out. *I did what was required.*

The creature lurches into the black pine forest again and again. Blood on its flank. Over fine bone china, the old lady laughs.

70.

In two weeks the place has become utterly strange again. He takes at least three wrong turns, and finds himself at the end of a corridor, a lift the only way out, and no stairs in sight. He doesn't usually take lifts. He stares hard at himself in the mirror, trying to see what his big face might hold beyond the familiar ugliness. A glimpse of his brother around the eyes, but that is about all. He feels presumptuous and insignificant.

The door opens for the top floor and he steps out into a white corridor he knows. He had left at first light, his mother and Lina still sleeping, and it is barely seven now. Everything feels unnaturally quiet. He turns to make for the room at the end of the corridor, and stops short.

She is walking precariously towards him, as if on a tightrope stretched across an abyss, one step at a time, wholly focused on the next few inches ahead. Her red hair is cropped tight around her face; her cheekbones are sharp, there are dark pools around her eyes. The drop on either side of her is terrifying, but all he can do is hold his breath and watch.

She sees him, or seems to, but she barely reacts, concentrating harder than ever, foot after careful foot, on the taut line. He can only wait, willing her on, readying himself to run forward if she should start to fall. She doesn't fall, though he can see that she is tiring. The effort of balance. The effort of moving forward. He is as patient as a mountain. He must not, he will not move.

Closer now, and the strain on her thin face is breaking him. Almost close enough, but not quite, she wobbles, breathes fast as a cat, but finds her balance, and keeps on.

At last she lifts her head and looks right at him, gives a small shout of triumph and holds out both her hands. He grasps them and pulls her in to him, away from the edge of the cliff.

Myra agrees to go back to bed and rest for a couple of hours, while Theo goes into organisational overdrive, vanquishing doctors, cajoling nurses, and battling for the necessary paperwork to get her released. Nobody, apart from Myra, thinks he's doing remotely the right thing, and it is only when she tells the Scottish consultant that she will simply stop eating if she cannot leave that people start to relent. A nurse shows them how to administer the current medication; a doctor makes them promise to return for further tests in a week. They agree unreservedly, and are finally left in peace to pack Myra's few possessions into her bag.

She takes an unemotional leave of the big gull on the roof outside her window. It has watched them intently throughout. Though if it wasn't for him, she says, I wouldn't have been up and walking so early this morning. He was beating against the pane when I woke up, it was horrible, I thought, I can't stay here, I have to get out...

A nurse arrives with Theo's letter. Myra opens it and looks hugely pleased.

My mother did the dragonflies, he says.

Come on then, she says. If you really are going to show me this pond.

Her legs are still rather shaky and she has to lean on his arm, but they make it to reception where she sits down for five minutes to get her strength. The space is done out in an unnecessarily bracing combination of purple and orange; the sheer number of people moving around overwhelms her. She closes her eyes, and finds Theo's hand.

But the hand pulls away and he is suddenly on his feet, pushing through a knot of queuing people, calling out *Dan! Luke!*

And then he sees that Teddy is walking between them, holding a hand each. The child spots Theo before they do, and opens his mouth in pure delight, reaching out his arms. Theo scoops him up and swings him high. You're not *lost*, little man! he says.

They don't take much persuading. Piled into the white van, driving away from the city and out towards the hills, they describe how Luke found Teddy cold and deeply asleep, like a creature hibernating, in a corner of the museum downstairs from the main hall, a place roped off for months, unused, full of lockers and tables. The silence had been pressing so long against the outside wall it had seeped through the pores of the stone, or got in through a crack, and pooled deeply enough to trap him like an insect in a puddle. How the paramedics had warmed him and woken him very slowly in the back of the ambulance, and how the hospital tests had found nothing wrong at all, and that this morning after a good sleep and a good breakfast they'd said it was OK to go.

So we went, says Luke happily.

Us too, says Myra, though they weren't quite so keen to let us out. The outside world comes at her too quickly, and she closes her eyes, feels Theo rejoicing beside her at the wheel.

Lina won't believe this, says Theo. We are going to celebrate for days and days.

I promised him pancakes, says Dan, stroking Teddy's head. He doesn't want to tell the others about the one thing that isn't quite right.

Mountains of pancakes, says Theo. Excellent idea. We'll need eggs.

71.

Lina had half woken to the sound of the van's tyres on the gravel under her window, and slept again. When she woke properly it was to sunlight and the chatter of small birds. Now she sits up in bed and feels the ache in her legs as something almost voluptuous. No need to move yet, the house is very quiet.

The room has a high ceiling and a large bay window and feels spacious in spite of the books and the pictures and the boxes piled everywhere. The furniture is eclectic and battered, but nicely shaped. She fingers the patchwork counterpane, intricate and faded, runs her finger along the neat little stitches and thinks of her mother.

The shoebox sits on the table. If you're sure, he had said after their long talk, and gone hunting up in the attic room for ages. This morning she doesn't know if she is sure.

After a while she slips out of bed and goes to the window, pulls open the curtains, and looks down over a garden of roses and fruit trees hung with small apples and ripe plums. Beyond it a track leads down to the open land, and to the sunlit pond. If Mrs Evans is strong enough, she thinks, they could go out and collect some plums to stew for when Myra comes. And she must see if there is anything in the kitchen cupboards to make a cake.

She decides she needs tea. Passing the room downstairs where Theo's mother sleeps she stops and listens to her breathing, deep and regular. In the kitchen she boils the kettle and hunts through cupboards. She finds yeast and olive oil and the right kind of flour, and mixes up some bread dough for later on. Cake looks like a possibility too, though she will need to find eggs. But not yet. She takes her tea back up to her room and sits down at the table with the box in front of her, tracing a wavy line through the dust on the lid with a fingertip. She lifts it off. Photos and letters are packed flat, in bundles; she picks one out and carefully unrolls the perished elastic band, which snaps. Then she spreads the dozen or so photos across the table without looking at them properly. She covers her face with her hands and closes her eyes in something like prayer. Eventually, she looks at them.

They are pictures from the past, from her past, from streets she could have known and might have recognised if they were not all so generically bombed and jagged, with figures in them she could have passed at any time, held in their moment in black and white. Children in doorways, with inscrutable expressions, looking straight at the camera. A woman carries a bag of groceries past a pile of rubble. A young father and a small boy sit side by side on a kerb. People you see every day on the news, her people; the dates on the back tell her how old this news is now. With a kind of detached curiosity she examines each picture, and whether or not they are looking back at her she acknowledges each person she sees, and passes on.

The next bundle is harder to look at. It documents the immediate aftermath of a bomb in a marketplace. This she does recognise, both the place and the event. A few streets away from them; she sometimes went there with the children for fruit and vegetables. Not that day, however. Ali had treated some of the wounded. The sister of a close friend of theirs had been among the dead. About a year before the end, she thinks, looking at the dates again; she would not have thought it so long.

Each photograph receives the same careful acknowledgment, an internal nod that is neither a prayer nor a blessing nor a farewell. There is no rage or pity in it either, and nothing that comes close to acceptance, but it is something she has learned to do, a way of looking that faces down horror. She wonders about the man behind the camera, whether he looked like Theo, whether he slept in this room when he was growing up. When she finishes this batch of pictures she gets up to open the window and finds that her hands are shaking.

Noises in the house, a toilet flushing, a door closing. Lina remembers her bread and goes down to the kitchen to knead the dough and put the kettle on. After a while Theo's mother appears in the doorway and smiles at her. Good morning, she says. I slept a long time.

Tea, Mrs Evans, says Lina. It's another lovely day, look. What shall we have for breakfast?

The morning goes quickly. They pick a bowlful of dark red plums and stew them with cinnamon. They can't find eggs, so make biscuits instead. The smell of bread fills the house. Lina retrieves her clothes from the washing machine and hangs them on the line. They drink coffee on a bench at the top of the garden, and Lina explains every so often where Theo has gone. Each time she tells her, the older woman looks pleased and surprised to hear he has gone to collect another friend. Then she wonders again where her other son has got to, and Lina says he is still away.

By late morning Mrs Evans is tired, and falls asleep in the green chair. Lina goes back upstairs to her room and works her way slowly through the last two bundles of photographs. In the last pile she finds a picture of a hospital in ruins; there are no people in this picture, and the place it so wrecked it could be anywhere; but the date on the back, she sees, is perfectly correct. That must be our hospital, she thinks, and he must be in there, deep in the rubble. It is, she knows now, the closest she will get.

72.

He swirls the pale mixture to cover the pan, and waits attentively for the rash of tiny dark air-pockets to appear. Then he slides the spatula underneath the pancake and feels it lift away nicely. Good pan, he thinks. Better than the flimsy thing at Luke's place. He flips it over and studies the surface of the moon. It is different every single time, the channels and veins, the rough patches where water might once have been, the craters and mounds; golden-brown skeins mapped onto a rich pale yellow, those lovely eggs from the farm shop just outside the village.

Lina comes in with a plate, laughing. He's finished it already, she says. You have to give him that one too.

This is Luke's, says Dan, firmly. Strict rotation. He was up all night too, you know...

He slides the pancake on to her waiting plate.

Teddy's, she says. He's starving. Or they'll have to share.

Whatever you do, says Dan, don't cut it in half or there'll be hell to pay. He goes berserk if you try and cut them in half.

Though quite how, he thinks, even Teddy might pull off a major tantrum in his current condition he isn't sure. He is briefly amused by the thought of his son silently jumping up and down like an angry cartoon character with the sound turned off. Then he thinks he would give anything to hear him scream.

Luke is next in.

This one's yours for definite, says Dan, flipping another moon.

Good, says Luke. Thought I'd come and make sure no one else intercepts it.

He walks up and down the kitchen holding his phone at peculiar angles, as if dousing for water.

I can't, ah, get a signal anywhere, he says.

You won't, calls Theo. Not in the house.

I need to tell work where I am; there's a meeting I'm going to miss.

Theo comes through. Land-line, he says, or email upstairs, it's usually pretty reliable. I can get you set up if you like.

You eat this first, says Dan.

After a while Lina persuades Dan that she can be trusted with the pan, and he joins Theo and his mother at the table. Teddy scrambles down off his chair and up into his lap. Myra, still dizzy from her tight-rope act, is propped up on the sofa eating her third pancake, and Luke has disappeared. They pour him tea and let him eat, and when Lina comes in with the last of the pancakes he tells them what they all know by now, which is that Teddy has no voice.

Otherwise he's fine. And he doesn't seem to know i
himself; it's not as though he's stopped talking...

Theo has found a book about birds, and Teddy is reading it very earnestly on the rug. Aloud, by the look of him
Invisible words.

Dak-dak, says Dan, automatically, encouragingly.

Is it just the shock of being lost? says Myra. A sort of re-
action? It might wear off, it's still very soon.

Dan nods. That's what I think, he says. Like losing your
voice. It'll come back, I'm sure.

Theo watches the silent talking child and says nothing.

Luke comes downstairs looking concerned. I, ah, have
to go, he says. At least, that is, if it's convenient for me to
go... There's something badly wrong at work, the professor
I need to see him, he's been ill. He's never ill. But I can, ah,
ring for a taxi?

I can give you a lift to the station, says Theo. I'll need to
buy supplies if this lot are staying. Dan looks at Luke, and
then at Lina who is down on the mat cross-legged with
Teddy tucked into her lap, pointing out the birds.

Stay here, says Luke. It's the best place for him. For both
of you. How about I, ah, come back tomorrow around sup-
pertime, if everything is sorted by then?

He turns to Theo. You sure that's OK?

Perfect. Let's go. There's a train at half-past you'll get,
no problem.

Luke says goodbye, and rubs Teddy's head. Then he remembers.

The, ah, city map upstairs on your wall? he says to Theo.
With the pools and the dates all marked on it?

Mmm, says Theo, hunting for keys.

Could I just take a quick picture of it? I have an idea...

Of course. Go ahead. I'll be in the van.

Theo crouches down beside Myra and cups her face in his big hands. Go upstairs and rest, he says. Lina will show you where. Go and lie down, have a sleep. I won't be long.

She closes her eyes and he kisses her lightly on the forehead, and when she opens them again he is gone.

73.

He is standing looking into the fridge when the doorbell rings. There is nothing there he could possibly eat. He tries the food cupboard, but it appears even less promising; everything in it is too dry or too complicated. The bell rings again. He crouches down and goes through a small stockpile of tins of tomatoes, lentils, and some water-chestnuts. He knows he must eat but has no hunger for anything he sees. He tries to imagine what he would choose, given the choice, but nothing occurs to him. In the end he dissolves a spoonful of honey into boiling water and sits at the kitchen table stirring it round and round and breathing in the steam.

The noise of the doorbell has been getting more insistent, but he has not, until now, been able to give it much attention. He wonders how the person outside knows he is inside, knows to keep ringing like that, and not give up and go away. It wouldn't make much sense, that level of persistence, he thinks, unless you knew for sure that someone might eventually answer.

He has a sip of honeyed water and begins to find the ringing profoundly annoying. Another couple of sips, and he realises that the only way to make it stop is to go all the way to the front door and ask the person doing it to go away. He heads unsteadily down the corridor and leans up against the door, shouting, please go away. I can't answer the door. I'm ill.

Sir, says a muffled voice. Sir. Please.

No sirs no pleases, he says. Just go away. I'm going back to bed.

The letterbox rattles and opens. The voice is clearer now, and familiar.

Sir, it's me, Luke. We, ah, need your help.

I can't help. I'm ill, for god's sake.

You have to; it's important.

I'm ill. I can't help. He sounds petulant, even to himself. At least the ringing has stopped.

Look, I can't help now, he says, being placatory. My legs won't hold up much longer. Come back another time.

I have a new map, says Luke. Your department is imploding. The silence, the interference is getting worse. A child nearly died. Sir, we have to do something. Please, just let me in, I need to explain what's going on. I think I've had an idea but I need to talk to you.

I've done everything I can, he says bitterly, and more.

Let me in, sir, says Luke, or I'll, ah, just keep ringing.

The professor thinks about this for a moment, then unlatches the door and lets him in.

Luke is shocked. The man who opens the door in his t-shirt and boxers is thin and unshaven, hollow-eyed. He looks at Luke standing on the doorstep with complete indifference.

The ringing, he says, was horrible. You'd better come in.

Luke says nothing, and follows him back to the kitchen, where the professor sits down to his mug of hot water and carries on stirring it, and sipping. He feels nervous.

How, ah, long have you been like this?

The professor brushes the words away with a delicate impatient hand.

Days, he says. I don't know. Tell me what you have to tell me. Then go away, I need to go back to bed.

Luke gets his iPad out and lays it on the table in front of him. He starts to explain, a little awkwardly at first, but warming, about the incident with Teddy, and what Phoebe had told him about the meeting in the department he had missed this afternoon, omitting the rumours of the professor's possible suspension, and then he starts to tell him about Theo's map with the ponds; but when he glances up he sees that the man at the other end of the table is trembling, shivering like an animal. Luke swallows the last of his residual fear and, still talking softly about the maps, moves round the table and puts a hand on the older man's shoulder, gently persuading him up onto his feet and out through to the bedroom at the back of the flat. He gets him to lie down, and quietly picks up the pile of keys from the bedside table.

I'm coming back, sir, he says. No ringing this time; if you could maybe just sleep a little now, I'll be back as soon as I can, OK?

The indifferent eyes look into him, through him, and then the man in the bed turns over to face the wall.

Luke pads around the flat, mildly surprised that it isn't bigger, and investigates the medicine cabinet, the fridge, the food cupboard. He makes a mental list, then slips out into the warm dark evening to hunt for supplies.

All is quiet on his return. He goes into the kitchen and starts to slice and fry onion and potatoes; he cuts and squeezes oranges, opens a bottle of red wine and finds himself a glass; emails Dan, just in case he's connected, and turns over maps in his head, nudging his way towards an idea which still refuses to come clear. Fresh juice; paracetamol; watercress soup.

A figure appears in the doorway. There is a little more life in his eyes.

That smells good, he says. I could eat some of that.

74.

He has pulled an armchair over to be closer to the bed, and now he sits with his eyes shut, thinking and not thinking. Late afternoon sun, August sun with the feel of September in it already, fills the room and falls on the table and the dusty shoebox, on the medicine bottles, the needles, the strips of pills. Myra lies deep asleep on Lina's bed. He is still concerned by what happens to her in sleep, and insists to Lina that they both watch her, taking turns. The watching is a rest from the work on the top floor and down the corridor, a great activity, all of them helping, clearing and cleaning rooms so that everyone will have a bed tonight.

There is no shortage of rooms in this house, but the accumulation of boxes of papers, books, odd items of furniture and a lifetime of his mother's paintings and sculptures has covered beds and sofas, and made spare mattresses inaccessible. Dan and Teddy have taken over the spacious attic room, hoovering and scrubbing and brushing away cobwebs, at least until distracted by the discovery of a box full of wooden blocks and animals. Lina is sorting out another bed in the smaller middle room, shifting piles of books into Theo's study and going through the linen cupboard for bedding.

Every so often Theo opens his eyes to watch Myra sleep. Then he drifts back down to the problem, the complex knot of thoughts and feelings lodged inside him, a tightness that even the quiet breathing of the woman on the bed cannot dissolve. We are not safe yet. He can see, now, that he had been wrong to think the silence could not reach them in the hills. He pictures the tendrils of nothingness spreading through his mother's mind, cutting off the old pathways, leaving her sentences with nowhere to go. And he feels again the comfortable weight of Teddy on his shoulders, the smooth, sturdy little legs held tight in his grasp. Heading down to the pond for a run around, while Lina and Dan went through the shopping and devised dishes for the evening; he could feel the child's delight through his body, but only guess at his silent commentary on the things he saw. Now and again he had thrown words into the conversation, hoping he was making sense.

Myra stirs and he sees fear flicker briefly across her face. The knot tightens, because he knows, at some level, that none of this will get better of its own accord, and that for Teddy to speak and for Myra to get properly well they will have to tackle the silence at its source. With his eyes closed he circles the knot in his mind, tugs at it, tries to loosen it, to get at its constituent threads.

Lina comes in holding a book bound in dark green leather. She smiles and beckons him over to the window. Look, she whispers, look what I found in the middle room.

It is a copy of the published Transactions of some lengthily titled scientific society, volume seventeen, it says in Roman numerals picked out in gold: 1863-4. He runs a finger down the spine and then sniffs the binding. Mmm, he says, childhood smell. What did you find?

She opens the volume on the table and flicks through the pages. Here, she says, long review of Haeckel, with some of the prints reproduced, look, aren't they beautiful? They were what got me started, all those years ago.

He turns the pages and looks at the line drawings of the Radiolaria, their delicate alien forms. I bet there's a copy of Haeckel here somewhere, he says. In my grandfather's library, nothing would surprise me.

She puts a finger to her mouth and glances at Myra. I'll come and sit now, and read this, she says, but can you help me first with the sheets? I have no idea which ones to use.

He makes a wry face and shrugs. Me neither, he says, but I'll try. Where's Mam now?

Drawing, says Lina. Downstairs drawing. Come on.

They leave quietly. A white butterfly with orange-tipped wings gets in through the open sash window and lands on the cardboard box in an infinitely subtle disturbance of dust. Myra stirs again, her eyelids flickering, trying to pull herself free of another dream where she is walking among rows and rows of war memorials, all bone-white and as monumental as her building, inscribed with names she cannot read, looking for something, avoiding someone, the old fear keeping her walking briskly, not looking back. The eyelids flicker again and open; the room is full of yellow light.

She lies still for a while until the rows of pale stone fade, and then she pulls herself to a sitting position and takes stock of her probable strength, her probable balance. She decides it is worth a go.

The butterfly is hurling itself against the glass of the lower window. An inch or two higher, she sees, and it would be away. Very carefully, she makes her way over to help, and cups it in her hands, feeling it flutter then go still. She throws it to its freedom and it dances off.

Turning for the door, she sees Lina's *Transactions* open on the table beside her; the line-drawings catch her eye. She turns a page in curiosity and freezes at what she sees; fragile and hanging, a fretted and many-pointed star. She finds a chair and sits down, flooded with disbelief.

75.

The house absorbs them, one by one. After the long meal, and the long conversations into the night, they find their way to the various new-made beds. Dan scoops Teddy off the rug and climbs up to the big mattress on the attic room floor. He leaves the window open for any stars that might be passing overhead. Lina kisses Myra, who has been quiet and distant all evening, and goes upstairs to her article. She falls asleep reading.

Myra is struggling to stay awake.

You're done in, says Theo, sitting down beside her on the sofa and taking her hand. You going up?

She shakes her head.

You should sleep, he says. Come on, I'll help you upstairs.

I'm not tired.

This is so patently untrue he laughs.

I'm not, she says, defiantly.

OK. You're not. What shall we do?

I need to stay awake, she says. Can we go outside?

He doesn't ask why she needs to stay awake, but hunts around underneath her till he finds one of her tucked-in feet. He measures it against his hand.

Wait here, he says. I'll see what I can do.

He disappears out the back somewhere and returns with a pair of his mother's boots and two pairs of thick socks.

City girl, he says. You can't go down to the pond in the dark in heels. You'll fall in.

She grins, and pulls the boots on, and then takes his arm.

There's a moon, he says. We might not even need the torch. Come on.

Down by the water there are all kinds of noises. Chirps and whistling and rustles, and the sound of something dropping into the water.

Are your frogs going to sing? she asks.

I doubt it, he says. Not the right time for it. Then he laughs.

Paddock moon, he says.

Mmm?

Pennant. The one that isn't mad; I mean not mad like Fort. He's mad in a good way, eighteenth-century mad. He's got a nice bit on frogs going quiet; *there is a time of year when they become mute, neither croaking nor opening their mouths for a whole month*. It's called the Paddock Moon, apparently.

Why?

192

Paddock means big frog.

I might have guessed.

Quite. *I am informed that for that period, their mouths are so closed, that no force (without killing the animal) will be capable of opening them...*

Is it true?

Of course not.

She thinks of hundreds of stubbornly mute frogs, their wide mouths clamped tight shut, watching them from the reeds and the muddy edges of the pond as they walk like giants slowly through the peculiar washed-out landscape; it is light enough to see the shapes of the hills across the marsh. The moon, the paddock moon, is huge and reflected. A late bat skims across them and dips down towards the pale water.

They stop to listen to the stream at the bottom of the pond, trickling out and down away towards the river. Not much there now, he says, it's been so hot. Wait till October, it's a proper cataract then.

All this, she says. It feels quite unreal. But then I wasn't brought up to it, I suppose.

How long were you in London? he asks.

Years, she says, brusquely. I came back when Mum got ill.

What did you do?

Model, she says, even brusquer. It is clear he will learn no more.

He gives her a hand over the stream.

You're right, though, he says. Doesn't matter how well you know somewhere, this light would make it unreal. It's like being inside a dream.

She shakes her head. Not one of mine she says, bitterly.

My dreams are rarely like this.

I know, he says, hugging her gently. I've seen you at it. Is that why you need to stay awake?

She shivers, folds herself into his arms.

Tell me, he says. Try and tell me, go on.

I think, she says, muffled, her face buried in his shirt, I think I'm going mad.

But not, he says softly, in a good way?

No, she says. In a frightening way.

Why?

I dream things, and then I see them; as if I've made them happen. That's not right.

Tell me.

She describes the frozen star in the book on the table. I dreamed it exactly, made of glass, weeks ago, in the hospital. It was terrible. What is it doing here?

Lina's Radiolaria, he says, reasonably. Beautiful things. Why was it terrible?

She won't say; she shakes her head impatiently. And then I come downstairs, she says, and I see your mother's drawings on the table, and there's the woman lying naked, and the face all made of spheres, and I dreamed them too, in the hospital, and that can't be right, and so I'm going mad, and I'll have to go back there, or worse, and I thought it was all, suddenly, going to be so much so much so much better... She is sobbing now, a whole evening of tension released in tears. He holds her tight and strokes her cropped hair and her wet cheeks and lets her cry.

You, he says, are not even eighteenth-century mad. You are far and away the sanest person I have ever met.

Later, as she lies curled up fast asleep in the small room off the study he sits and thinks, and searches through his mind for clues. And after a long while he remembers the name, Galatea, and he sets off hunting through the internet, chasing lines of text and images out in the far reaches of cyberspace.

76.

He calls in discreetly at the office to copy files from a computer, and then at his flat to change and shower and pick up clean clothes and nappies and Teddy's manky old rabbit, who is sorely missed. Then he heads down to the station, and waits for the next train with a coffee and a sandwich, feeling the gathering energy inside him as his ideas gather shape.

He had slept on the sofa at the professor's flat, and made him a Californian breakfast, piles of fresh fruit with granola, and yoghurt and honey, and a small strong coffee that visibly shook him awake. Then, while the older man showered, he had changed the sweat-soaked sheets and made up the bed again, opening windows, letting in the bright air. They had continued last night's conversation, and after looking through maps and hearing more about the situation in the university, the professor had finally been persuaded to face some of the messages piled up inside his phone. Between them, for over an hour, they had worked out an immediate strategy to get round the lock-down on their project. Luke had shown him, in more detail, Theo's map with all the ponds; and the professor had told Luke, very briefly, and before a new rush of fatigue had sent him back to bed, about the unofficial deal with the castle.

We have about a fortnight, he said. God, I need my strength back for this.

Luke stares with some interest at the electronic notice-board and notes the number of trains delayed and cancelled, and wonders if this is a new development, or an old one worsening, and whether the interference is involved here too. He can ask Theo, he supposes, he would know. Looking down to check that both of his bags are under the bench, he sees the rabbit's ears poking out of his knapsack. Feeling slightly self-conscious, though no one at all is watching, he pushes them further in.

A couple of hours later the rabbit is the first thing to be pulled out of the bag; the sheer force of Teddy's mute delight makes them all clap and shout.

Though why, says Luke, it is a rabbit and not a bear I still don't know.

Oh there were bears enough when he was born, says Dan, pouring him a glass of wine; but it'd be confusing to have another Teddy around.

Isn't Theo one? says Luke, I mean, aren't you both named after Roosevelt? Theodore?

Nope, says Dan. Ted Hughes.

Theophilus, says Theo.

Bloody hell.

I know. Don't tell anyone. Family name. A proud line of obsessives.

Myra is on the sofa, shaking with laughter.

You can't possibly...

I can, he says. And I am.

They cook and eat, and afterwards clear the table for a council of war. Theo fetches the big wall map down from his study, and spreads it out, pinning down its corners with half-drunk glasses and coffee cups and mugs of peppermint tea.

Well, he says. Tell us.

And Luke tells them, carefully and slowly, everything he now knows and everything he has thought of since yesterday. Theo looks at him in admiration.

That, he says, is one hell of a plan. I was only halfway there; I can't believe you've got us access.

Are you sure, says Dan, about the deal with the castle? I mean, do you know if the Scottish lot really have any power? I thought ButeCo was pretty well just a corporate entity; I assumed they'd bought, or you know, just retained, the use of the name... Can they really grant access? If the official line is so dead set against anyone even mentioning the castle?

Luke shrugs. The professor wouldn't say much about what, ah, happened up there. Just that he's been, and that they do have access, for this performance, those three days. One to set up and rehearse – it's complex stuff, apparently, and then some kind of, ah, special showing, on the second night for them, for the family and anyone they care to invite. And then a day to take it all down.

It is complex, says Myra, incredibly complex; I saw them in London about ten years ago, they were astonishing. She was still dancing then. Do we get to watch too? Have you met her?

Luke shakes his head. No, he says. Never. But I don't see why we shouldn't get ourselves invited.

So suppose, says Theo, pulling them back to the problem. Suppose we do have access, for those three days. What then?

Luke laughs. Ah, you know what then, he says. You know perfectly well what then.

Lot of work, though, says Theo, shaking his head. But then we won't get another chance like this.

Dan looks at them both, and again at the two maps, and suddenly gets it. He grins triumphantly round the table.

Teddy and I, he says, know a man with a digger.

77.

There were not so many messages, in the end. She is too proud to persist, he thinks, to keep flinging herself at my inbox. Fair enough. She doesn't do melodrama. The unread texts cluster at the bottom of the list; ten days ago, a week. Then nothing at all. There doesn't seem much point in reading them now.

He does not know what to think, or what to do. Apologise. Make excuses. I was protecting you. I didn't want to infect you. I was ashamed. Of course he wishes he had woken out of the nightmare to coffee and yoghurt and piles of fresh fruit and sunlight and her. But he is a realist, and hardly such a fool as to think that a handful of unanswered messages might bring her running the length of Wales, leaving her performers dangling in mid-air from their silken ropes.

Although, he thinks, I could have thrown myself off Ben

bloody Nevis a week ago and you, my love, would be absolutely none the wiser.

Nonetheless, he has to know if she is still coming.

He shaves, and glares at the man who emerges. The man glares back. He dresses properly, for the first time since staggering home from the station. Then he makes himself a coffee and cuts a slice of fresh bread, blessing Luke for the hundredth time, and sits at the kitchen table wondering what on earth to say that will not sound trite or self-pitying or off-hand. In the end all he does is write her name, Meg, and press send. Then he pushes his hands hard against his eyes to try and stop tears forcing their way through the closed lids.

When he opens his eyes again there is a response.

Yma.

He smiles in spite of himself. No you're not, he thinks. But this will do.

He asks if she is still coming. Yes, she says, yes, it's shaping now. They will travel down on the nineteenth; they need accommodation for seven people and parking for two lorries. And can the university or the castle supply the seating?

He cannot tell her how far he is from being able to organise anything. That he is as weak and directionless as an animal that has lost pints of blood; that he knows now for certain he has no power at work anymore; a brusque email from HR has confirmed his suspension. But he thinks of Luke, and Luke's friends, and promises her that these things will be done.

Diolch, he adds, after a while. *Diolch.*

There is silence from her end, and then she asks: *Ti'n iawn?*

He sips his coffee and thinks about the question.
No, he replies. Not really.
I thought not.
They leave it at that.

78.

There are indeed, he finds, discreet, almost beautiful rolls
of tiny metal spikes woven all along the tops of the railings
and the mossy stone walls. He hunts out the old places,
where the bent and buckled metal used to let him in and
out, and finds only lines of neat, straight bars. The gates
and doors have new swipelocks fitted. They really have
been busy, he thinks, this last month or so. But thank god
they are not finished quite yet: there is one last place where
Luke can climb over later on. He's nervous, of course.
Afraid he'll fuck up the controls, run amok, wake the
neighbours: police cars *and* diggers, imagine how thrilled
Teddy would be. Wishes he had Theo to defer to. But
they've all agreed this is the best chance they'll get, before
the Parks work is done and Rhod moves on. The machines
themselves are still around, clustered for the night up near
the offices, behind the big information display set up by the
Parks and Gardens Charitable Foundation, who have gone
to no end of trouble to engage with the public and explain

in words and pictures, in numbers and diagrams, how vastly improved the Citizen Park Experience will soon be.

They had all come in earlier that afternoon in the van, dropping Myra at her flat to collect more clothes. She would stay in town tonight, she said, and sort a few things out. Theo had finally persuaded his mother to try the wheelchair, and with Lina pushing Teddy in the buggy they had walked along the river in a rich yellow light and had tea in one of the cafes, and admired the massed bright daisies and the scented roses. Then they had found a spot behind the castle, far enough away to be out of the cold, and spread out a couple of blankets, settling down to read and nap and unobtrusively explore the area foot by careful foot, translating the maps and the sketches made that morning into features on the ground. Luke, in a high-viz jacket, had produced a clipboard and scrambled down to take pictures of the emptied external moat. Dan and Teddy went off to look for Rhod.

Digger! said Rhod enthusiastically, holding Teddy on his lap so Dan could climb up to join them. *Yellow digger!* You're driving it, mate! Look at you go now – go on, say *digger*, then, there's a lad.

He's not saying anything these days, said Dan, and told him why.

Bastards, said Rhod, with non-specific disdain. What's a little man like that ever done to them?

He fished a key out of his jacket pocket.

As promised; got you this. It's a copy. All yours. And the pipes are in the back here. I'd do it myself but my job's already on the line. You know what to do? You got help?

Yes, said Dan. I know what to do. And I have got help. When's best, do you think?

I reckon about one. Nobody on site after midnight and they don't come back before five or six. Good luck.

Teddy had gone home in the van with Lina and Theo and Mrs Evans. Covered in ice-cream. Barely a backward glance. Dan grins into the darkness and tries to imagine how they've managed with bedtime. The closing-time alarm has been and gone; the sun has gone down, and the sweepers and their dogs have done the rounds for drunks and druggies and anybody considering committing lewd acts in a public place. He lies curled on the floor of the digger cab and wonders where they all go these days, the people who used to break into Eden after dark.

Now Dan has the entire park to himself, and finds that his eyes can manage with the light from the city and the last chunk of a waning moon, and the stars. He walks. The concrete path is clear enough. Something large and indistinguishable crosses swiftly into a dark mass of trees up ahead. He isn't afraid. *Out in the dark,* he thinks. Though it isn't snowing, of course. Still, out in the dark, the fallow doe... *fast as the stars are slow.*

He walks and walks to keep warm, to keep awake, and imagines that it is years ago, and that he can feel Jane's cold slim hand in his. Always cold, her hands. And that she is pulling him across the wet short grass of the rugby pitch to find a good open place for them to spread their coats and lie on their backs and look at the stars. Lesson One, she says, the Plough. And from there follow my finger to the Pole Star. And from there, she says, I can take you anywhere.

79.

Did she, or you, never get them in some kind of order?

Theo considers. It's a sort of archaeological order, he says. You go down levels. That's what I'm doing now.

She sits on the table in his study, watching him hunt through the stacks of paintings and drawings leant up against the far wall.

There are dates on some, he says. Though not all. You're right. It is a bit chaotic.

What you should do, she says, is take photos of them all individually, and number them, and wrap and store them somewhere safe. Then you'd have them all on the computer and you'd know where they were, if ever you need them.

She pauses for a split second, then says, with a flicker of mischief, to his crouched back, you know, like water-beetles. Properly catalogued.

He ignores the beetles. Too many pictures, he says. It would take ages. I don't have time. He straightens up briefly, and then hunkers down again, still searching.

I do, she says. And I like your mother's stuff. I could do it, slowly, a few at a time. And I think she could even sell some of them online... I'm fed up with doing nothing. And I'm not going back to work.

No? he says, looking up at her in surprise. Since when?

Since a few days ago. I phoned my boss. If I leave, there's more chance they'll keep Elin. And I get a reasonable deal. I'll be fine for a few months; the flat isn't too bad. I paid off a big chunk of mortgage when Mum died.

Hmm, he says. I could tell you that you're not supposed to make big life decisions when you're ill, but I don't suppose there's much point in me trying.

None whatsoever, she says, and flashes him a delighted smile.

He doesn't dare ask if that means she'll be staying a little while longer, a few days, a few weeks, forever. He keeps leafing through the layers, until at last he finds what he's looking for.

Look, Myra, he says. Look at this.

She flinches. Turns her head away.

He lays the picture flat on the table beside her, and puts an arm round her shoulders.

It's OK, he says, quietly. Come on, please look.

It is clearer, in this picture done in pastels and charcoal, that the woman is made of marble, as is the man with the neat curly beard who bends over her, possessive and tender, triumphant; he cannot see, beyond the curve of her hips and shoulders, the thin-lipped face with the eyes devoid of hope.

Myra shivers and closes her eyes.

Why, she says in a whisper, are you doing this?

See that date at the bottom of the page, he says evenly, ignoring her distress. She drew this twenty-five years ago, in the museum. There was an exhibition. You know who it is?

She shakes her head.

Galatea. And that's Pygmalion. He carves her, sculpts

204

her out of marble, to his own specifications, as it were. And she comes alive.

She's not happy, says Myra, grimly.

No, not in this one. There are others. Rodin did two at least; and Dali, that's your woman made of spheres, I don't know how the curator managed it, but she was by all accounts a seriously persuasive woman. International exhibition, major pieces, major pictures – bits of script and stills from productions of Shaw. Amazing thing. I found some old reviews online.

He looks her straight in the eyes.

You must have been there, Myra. You didn't make them up. You saw them in the museum when you were small...You'd have been, what...

Seven or eight, says Myra, gradually understanding. Perhaps. Perhaps I did.

You see, he says calmly. No madder than the rest of us.

She lets it sink in, and begins to feel relief, the slow, slow easing of knotted anxiety inside her.

And the glass thing?

Always been there. You could have seen that any time. Like the turtle.

She shakes her head. Not any time, she says, firmly. You know I don't go in. Not since I came back. And we left for London when I was nine.

She almost adds, but doesn't quite, *with the man*.

Instead she shakes everything out of her head and slips down off the table.

That's enough, now, she says. More than enough. Come on. I'm feeling strong today. You said you had a rowan tree to show me.

80.

It is mid-September, and they have arrived. On the first day they build the large circular stage across the moat and the flat grassy circle where the mound and the keep used to be. Then they construct the complex labyrinth of metal poles and lights and ropes and mirrors. Finally, they raise the huge white canvas marquee to cover it all, opened at one side to face the stands where the audience will sit. Luke realises, as the day wears on, that the cold will be a problem for the audience. It has already been a huge problem for the workers from the troupe, slowing everyone down, forcing them to find coats and gloves in local charity shops, and to stop every so often and climb up the steep grassy banks, or to go outside the castle walls altogether and rediscover warmth in the mellow September sun. The difficulty of performing even straightforward tasks in the thick of the silence tells on everybody. There are arguments; there are even tears, and by six o'clock Meg Vaughan looks at the washed-out, exhausted faces of her performers and sends them away to the hotel. Sleep, she signs, pulling the gloves from her cold hands to make herself clear. Go and find something to eat, go to the pub. Don't come back before ten tomorrow morning. We'll rehearse then. Go.

She beckons Luke over and gestures that they should climb the bank out of the worst of the silence. He has spent the day being helplessly star-struck and superbly efficient. He follows her with his heart beating a hint too fast. She has seen how quick he is with his iPad, and sits him down next to her, and leans across him, and writes:

Where is he?

Luke pulls a face. I don't know.

Ill?

Yes.

Too ill for this?

I think he will come. Will you write to him to ask?

She shakes her head, and shrugs. Not me.

He senses a deep complication, and nods. I'll go to the flat now, he taps, if you're sure...

She nods her head, and looks momentarily sad. Then sharper, determined. He's the only one talking to the family, she writes. Say it has to be him here, with her, on the night.

She looks down at the domed white canvas. How's it going, underneath?

Pretty good. Tiring. Bloody cold. We'll carry on tomorrow.

She nods, wearily.

Luke is suddenly overwhelmed by an incoherent rush of pity and tenderness and admiration, and begins typing furiously.

Professor Vaughan... I... I just wanted to say how much...

She puts one hand on his to stop him writing, and a finger on her silent lips, and shakes her head and smiles. Then she stands up and, without saying a thing, formally thanks him for his help and his work throughout the day. He bows his head and says good-bye, and goes off to talk to the professor.

On the morning of the second day Theo and Dan decide to open the cap on the pipe buried by the digger three weeks previously. They put a few orange bollards in neat lines, dig through the last layer of earth, and then stand in their official yellow jackets, with unconcerned faces and wildly excited hearts, watching the water pour in a nicely controlled stream from the Dock-feeder canal into the recently-drained external moat. The woman in the headscarf pushing a lively blond child, and the striking girl with short red hair helping an elderly lady along the path whoop unexpectedly, as if in celebration. The two officials merely frown, and pretend not to notice. The ditch fills slowly, but impressively, and by the afternoon the water reflects the sky and laps the walls as it has always done.

He comes in the evening when there is no choice; he comes when absolutely summoned. In a suit and a tie, with his winter coat and scarf over his arm. He is charming and beautiful. He drinks sherry with the rich and powerful in the Winter Smoking Room, where a myriad gilt stars and the entire zodiac riot above his head. She is not among them. *Omnia Vincit Amor*, he thinks. *So where are you now?* He avoids eye contact with the stuffed and antlered heads on the painted walls.

The old lady's hand curves like a claw around his arm as he helps her to her seat in the stand, tucks in the fake tartan blankets around her, and hands her a glass of gin. Then, like some sacrificial victim, he takes his place beside her and looks to the trailing sunset behind the towers as one might look to the promised land. The stars will strengthen, and move across the sky, he thinks, and eventually this night will be over.

The hand resting briefly on his other arm is Luke's. He clasps it, and thanks him again, and apologises under his breath for his unspeakable weakness. Luke reminds him to put his coat on.

Free-eezing, he says. I have to, ah, check the others. Good luck, sir.

He goes along the row to find Myra and Lina, and Mrs Evans, and Teddy, all bundled into too many clothes, with quilts and eiderdowns piled across their laps.

If you feel the cold is getting dangerous, he hisses, just *leave*, OK?

They nod, obedient. And the stage lights up.

The bodies twist and turn in constantly shifting light. They hang from the scaffolding and cables and ropes; they dance and somersault. One walks a metal wire. There are stories of encounters and oppressions and partings. Myra feels her cheeks wet with tears. The dancers' faces have a chalky, unearthly quality, and they perform in a depth of perfect silence they have never before, as a company, achieved. The strain it puts them under does not show.

And while they are absorbed in the figures on the stage, Lina and Myra find that two dark, wet and muddied bodies have crept into their row, and huddle shivering at their feet. They wrap them in eiderdowns and blankets, and hold their frozen hands to warm them. Myra wraps her silvery scarf around Theo's neck and runs her hands through his spiky wet hair. Below them, under the silk ropes and the pool of light, deep under the boards of the stage, the released water rises gradually in the empty space of the old moat.

On the third day the scaffolding comes down, and the

boards come up, but the white canvas dome remains, hiding the night's work for as long as possible from the man in the uniform at the door.

The professor wakes surprisingly late, and thinks with relief of the small private plane flying up the coast towards Scotland. And sees, over and over, the beautiful figure on the stage, bowing discreetly at the end of the performance and raising her face to everyone sat out there in the dark. It is an illusion, he remembers, to think that people on the stage are looking directly at you. The lorries are probably heading north by now, or wherever the next performance may be. He wonders if she has gone with them.

He heads into town down the river and thinks that whatever happens next he will not be here to see it. He plans to walk the length of the country, to the mountains in the north, and if she will see him, so be it. And if not, he can climb the mountains, and start to get himself well. He remembers that Luke's friend is looking for a flat, and is relieved to think he can be of some use there, at least.

There is a change inside the castle walls. The space is still as scraped bare as it ever was: still square, and still curiously emptied of its violent history, Romans, Normans, the army that destroyed the Chartists. But there is a loosening of the air.

He guesses that everyone is hidden inside the white tent. He pushes the canvas flap and finds a whole world inside: a deep circle of water, and the new island where a dozen people are busily planting trees.

81.

Theo parks the van at the far end of the museum car park. When he steps down onto the tarmac it is covered in yellow gingko leaves. He picks one up, a perfect specimen, and twirls the stem between his large thumb and middle finger. The air is November sharp.

She is sitting on the bench, waiting. He can see her red hair, grown enough already to curl down the nape of her neck, as he comes from the direction of the building. He sits beside her and puts the leaf in her hand.

I remember these, she says.

They are old, old, he says. Prehistoric.

He pulls a crumpled unopened letter out of his bag.

I have some results, he says. The star-shot.

She waves an official envelope, also unopened.

Me too, she says. Hospital.

Ah, he says. Do you want to open yours first, or shall I?

Neither, she says. I want to go in there.

Sure you're ready?

I'm sure.

Good plan, he says. We'll see the turtle. And the Blaschkas. And we can have coffee there as well.

She jumps up from the bench and holds out her hands

to pull him up. The silver bracelet glints on her wrist. He almost kisses her, but is distracted by a kestrel hovering above the castle.

Look at that, he says. There must be something worth having in there. Already. Mouse, perhaps.

She thinks of the mouse going about its business in the newly fallen leaves and wishes it luck. She wonders what else might end up living behind the square walls, given the chance, and whether the habitat would ever be suitable for aardvarks. She thinks of the slim, nearly dormant young trees, the rowans and the thorns and the hazels and the little oaks; and she thinks of the sleeping water, filled with tiny eggs and organisms, and imagines how busy the place will be come the spring.

Do you think it will last till spring? she asks. Do you think they'll let it stay?

He shrugs. If Luke can persuade them it was their idea all along, he says. Stranger things have happened. The silence didn't do them any good, after all, it just drew attention to all the other stuff they're up to; and they'll doubtless be glad to tell the world how green they are, how caring. That's a lot of hail-marys in there.

I can't wait to hear the frogs, she says. When they get their voices back. Imagine the racket.

He takes her by the hand and they walk past the little bronze girl, and cross the road, and climb the granite steps together: seven, then nine. And at the very top, just before the big door, where it clings like cold gossamer on their faces, they push together through the vestigial threads of the silence.

Rhag yr oerfel

Glossary of Welsh phrases

Aur a thus a myrr – Gold, frankincense and myrrh.

Pobl sy'n Eistedd ar Feinciau – People who Sit on Benches.

Be ti'n feddwl, Leusa? – What do you think, Leusa?

Dim rili yn... t'wbod. Dim rili yn gweithio... Dim imi, ta beth. Sori. – Doesn't really... you know. Doesn't really work... Not for me anyway. Sorry.

Bainc/mainc – both forms for 'bench'.

Un dau, un dau, un dau – one two, one two, one two.

Dere, dere nawr – come, come now.

annifyr – adjective covering a range: 'disagreeable/uneasy/unpleasant'.

Dim yn dy geg! – Not in your mouth!

ddim yn ffôl o gwbl t'wbod. Beth am Calon Lân? – Not a bad idea at all, you know. What about [the popular hymn] *Calon Lân?*

Ond mae pawb yn hoffi Calon Lân! – But everyone likes *Calon Lân!*

Ti ddim yn oer lan fan 'na ngwas i? – Aren't you cold up there, my boy?

Pob lwc – Good luck.

Bachgen mawr! – Big boy!

Wrth ymyl y degell – Next to the kettle.

Broga – frog.

Angen siarad – Need to talk.

Cneifio – shearing (sheep).

Yma – here.

Ti'n iawn? – Are you all right?

Acknowledgements

This book would not have been written without the support of a grant from Llenyddiaeth Cymru / Literature Wales: I am extremely grateful to them for helping me carve out the time to write it. Thanks too, are due to various people for help and inspiration along the way: to David Anderson and the staff at the National Museum of Wales, Cardiff; to Aled Gruffydd Jones and the staff at the National Library of Wales; to my editor Penny Thomas and all at Seren; to Paul Frame for conversations about Radiolaria, and to Gareth Griffith for (still inconclusive) conversations about star-jelly; to Si Constantine for introducing me to Rainer; to my parents, for Norrard, where parts of this were written; and to Liz Edwards, Margaret Ames and (as ever) David Parsons for moral support. Especial thanks are due to Clive Hicks-Jenkins for finding the time to produce the beautiful cover and illustrations; and to Peter Wakelin, for reading and commenting on the whole thing with amazing grace under difficult circumstances.

Direct citations in the text come from: Charles Fort, *The Book of the Damned* (1904); John Morton, *The Natural History of Northamptonshire* (1712); Thomas Pennant, *British Zoology* (1766); Edward Thomas, 'Out in the Dark'. Lines are quoted from Rainer Ptacek, 'Here I Am' (The Farm, 2002); lines from Bob Dylan's 'Seven Days' are quoted by kind permission of BD Music Company /Ram's Horn Music. All efforts have been made to trace copyright holders.